I0632562

Edmund Yates

The Yellow Flag

A Novel. Vol. III

Edmund Yates

The Yellow Flag
A Novel. Vol. III

ISBN/EAN: 9783337102685

Printed in Europe, USA, Canada, Australia, Japan

Cover: Foto ©Andreas Hilbeck / pixelio.de

More available books at **www.hansebooks.com**

THE YELLOW FLAG.

A Novel.

By EDMUND YATES,

AUTHOR OF 'A WAITING RACE,' 'BROKEN TO HARNESS,' ETC.

'That single effort by which we stop short in the downhill path to
perdition is itself a greater exertion of virtue than an hundred acts of
justice.' OLIVER GOLDSMITH.

IN THREE VOLUMES.

VOL. III.

LONDON:

TINSLEY BROTHERS, 18 CATHERINE ST. STRAND.

1872.

CONTENTS OF VOL. III.

THE YELLOW FLAG.

CHAPTER I.

ROSE COTTAGE TO LET.

IT was probably not without a certain amount of consideration and circumspection that John Calverley had fixed upon Hendon as the place in which to establish his second home, to which to take the pretty trusting girl who believed herself to be his wife. It was a locality in which she could live·retired, and in which there was very little chance of his being recognised. It offered no advantages to gentlemen engaged in the City—it was not accessible by either boat, 'bus, or rail; the pony-

carriages of the inhabitants were for the most
part confined to a radius of four miles in their
journeys, and Davis's coach and the carrier's
wagon were the sole means of communication with the metropolis.

Also, in his quiet, undemonstrative way,
Mr. Calverley had taken occasion to make
himself acquainted with the names, social
position, and antecedents of all the inhabitants, and to ascertain the chances of their
ever having seen or heard of him, which he
found on inquiry were very remote. They
were for the most part Hendon born and bred,
and the few settlers amongst them were retired tradesmen, who had some connection
with the place, and who were not likely, from
the nature of the business they had pursued
while engaged in commerce, to have become
acquainted with the person, or even to have
heard the name of the head of the firm in
Mincing-lane. About the doctor and the
clergyman, as being the persons with whom
he would most likely be brought into contact,
he was specially curious. But his anxiety

was appeased on learning that Mr. Broadbent was of a Devonshire family, and had practised in the neighbourhood of Tavistock previous to his purchase of old Doctor Fleeme's prac- tice ; while the vicar, Mr. Tomlinson, after leaving Oxford, had gone to a curacy near Durham, whence he had been transferred to Hendon.

So, when he had decided upon the house, and Alice had taken possession of it, John Calverley congratulated himself on having settled her down in a place where not merely he was unknown, but where the spirit of in- quisitiveness was unknown also. He heard of no gossiping, no inquiries as to who they were, or where they had come from. Com- ments, indeed, upon the disparity of years be- tween the married couple reached his ears ; but that he was prepared for, and did not mind, so long as Alice was loving and true to him. What cared he how often the world called him old, and wondered at her choice ?

It must be confessed that concerning the

amount of gossip talked about him and his household, John Calverley was very much deceived. The people of Hendon was not different from the people of any other place, and though they lived remote from the world, they were just as fond of talking about the affairs of their neighbours as fashionable women round the tea-table in their boudoirs, or fashionable men in the smoking-room of their clubs. They discussed Mrs. A.'s tantrums and Mrs. B.'s stinginess, the doctor's wife's jealousy, and the parson's wife's airs; all each others' shortcomings were regularly gone through, and it was not likely that the household at Rose Cottage would be suffered to escape. On the contrary, it was a standing topic, and a theme for infinite discussion. Not that there was the smallest doubt amongst the neighbours as to the propriety of Alice's conduct, or the least question about her being the old gentleman's wife, but the mere fact of Mr. Claxton's being an old gentleman, and having such a young and pretty wife, excited a vast amount of talk; and when it was found that Mr. Clax-

ton's business caused him to be constantly
absent from home, there was no end to the
speculation as to what that absence might not
give rise. There seemed to be some sort of
notion among the inhabitants that Alice would
some day be carried bodily away, and many
an innocent artist with his sketch-book in his
breast-pocket, looking about him in search of
a subject, has been put down by Miss M'Craw
and her friends as a dangerous character, full
of desperate designs upon Mr. Claxton's domestic happiness.

Miss M'Craw was a lady who took great
interest in her neighbours' affairs, having but
few of her own to attend to, and being naturally of an excitable and inquiring disposition,
she had made many advances towards Alice,
which had not been very warmly reciprocated,
and the consequence was that Miss M'Craw
devoted a large portion of her time to espion-
age over the Rose Cottage establishment, and
to commenting on what she gleaned in a very
vicious spirit. Early in the year in which the
village was startled by the news of Mr. Clax-

ton's death, Miss M'Craw was entertaining two or three of her special friends at tea in her little parlour, from the window of which she could command a distant view of the Rose Cottage garden gate, when the conversation, which had been somewhat flagging, happened to turn upon Alice, and thenceforth was carried on briskly.

'Now, my dear,' said Miss M'Craw, in pursuance of an observation she had previously made, 'we shall see whether he comes back again to-day. This is Wednesday, is it not? Well, he has been here for the last three Wednesdays, always just about the same time, between six and seven o'clock, and always doing the same thing.'

'Who is he? and what is it all about, Martha?' asked Mrs. Gannup, who had only just arrived, and who had been going through the ceremony known as 'taking off her things' in the little back parlour, while the previous conversation had been carried on.

'O, you were not here, Mrs. Gannup, and didn't hear what I said,' said Miss M'Craw.

'I was mentioning to these ladies that for the last three Wednesdays there has come a strange gentleman to our village, quite a gentleman too, riding on horseback, and with a groom behind him, well-dressed, and really,' added Miss M'Craw, with a simper, 'quite good-looking!'

She was the youngest of the party, being not more than forty-three years old, and in virtue of her youth was occasionally given to giggling and blushing in an innocent and play-ful manner.

'Never mind his good looks, Martha,' said one of the ladies, in an admonitory tone, 'tell Mrs. Gannup what you saw him do.'

'Always the same,' said Miss M'Craw. 'He always leaves the groom at some dis-tance behind him, and rides up by the side of the Claxtons' hedge, and sits on his horse staring over into their garden. If you wind up that old music-stool to the top of its screw,' continued the innocent damsel, 'and put it into that corner of the window, and move the bird-cage, by climbing on to it you can see a

bit of the Claxtons' lawn ; and each time that
I have seen this gentleman coming up the hill
I have put the stool like that and looked out.
Twice Mrs. Claxton was on the lawn, but
directly she saw the man staring at her she
ran into the house.'

'Who,' said Mrs. Gannup, 'who is she
that she should not be looked at as well as
anybody else ?   I hate such mock modesty!'

'And what I was saying before you came
in, dear,' cried Miss M'Craw, who fully agreed
with the sentiment just enunciated, 'was,
that this being Wednesday, perhaps he will
come again to-day.   I fixed our little meeting for to-night, in order that you might all
be here to see him in case he should come.
It is strange, to say the least of it, that a young
man should come for three weeks running
and stare in at a garden belonging to people
whom he does not know, at least, whom I suppose he does not know, for he has never made
an attempt to go to the front gate to be let in.'

'There is something about these Claxtons—' said Mrs. Gannup.

And the worthy lady was not permitted to finish her sentence, for Miss M'Craw, springing up from her chair, cried, 'There he is again, I declare, and punctual to the time I told you. Now bring the music-stool, quick!'

Her visitors crowded round the window, and saw a tall man with a long fair beard ride up to the hedge of the Claxtons' garden, as had been described by Miss M'Craw, rein-in his horse, and stand up in his stirrups to look over the hedge.

So far the programme had been carried out exactly, to the intense delight of the onlookers.

'Tell us,' cried Mrs. Gannup to Miss M'Craw, who was mounted on a music-stool, 'tell us, is she in the garden?

'She ! No,' cried Miss M'Craw, from her coigne of vantage, 'she is not, but he is. Mr. Claxton is walking up and down the lawn with his hands behind his back, and directly the man on horseback saw him he ducked down. See, he is off already!'

And as she spoke the rider turned his

horse's head, and, followed by his groom, cantered slowly away.

When he had gone for about a mile he reduced his horse's pace to a walk, and sitting
back in his saddle, indulged in a low, noise-
less, chuckling laugh.

'It was John Calverley; no doubt about
that,' he said to himself. 'I thought it was
he a fortnight ago, but this time I am sure of
it. Fancy that sedate old fellow, so highly
thought of in the City, one of the pillars of
British commerce, as they call him, spending
his spare time in that pretty box with that
lovely creature. From the glance I had of
her at the window just now she seems as be-
witching as ever. What a life for her, to be
relegated to the society of an old fogey like
that!—old enough to be her father, at the
very least, and knowing nothing except about
subjects in which she can scarcely be expected
to take much interest. Not much even of
that society, I should say; for old Calverley
still continues to live with his wife in Walpole-
street, and can only come out here occasion-

ally, of course. What a dull time she must have of it, this pretty bird! how she must long for some companionship! for instance, that of a man more of her own age, who has travelled, and who knows the world, and can amuse her, and treat her as she ought to be treated.'

Thus communing with himself, the good-looking, light-bearded gentleman rode on towards London, crossing the top of Hampstead Heath, and making his way by a narrow path, little frequented, but apparently well known to him, into the Finchley-road. There, close by the Swiss Cottage, he was joined by another equestrian; a gentleman equally well mounted and almost equally good-looking. This gentleman stared very much as he saw the first-named rider pass by the end of the side-road up which he was passing, and sticking spurs into his horse quickly came up with him.

' My dear Wetter,' he cried, after they had exchanged salutations, ' what an extraordinary fellow you are! You have still got the chestnut thoroughbred, I see; do you continue to like him?'

'I still have the chestnut thoroughbred,
and I continue to like him,' said Mr. Wetter
with a smile, 'though why I am an extraordinary fellow for that I am at a loss to perceive.'

'Not for that, of course,' said his friend;
'that was merely said par parenthèse. You
are an extraordinary fellow because one never
sees you in the Park, or in any place of that
sort, and because one finds you riding alone
here, evidently on your way back from some
outlandish place in the north-west. After
grinding away in the City, and wearying your
brain, as you must do, with your enormous
business, one would think you would like a
little relaxation.'

'It is precisely because I do grind away
all the day in the City, I do weary my brain,
I do want a little relaxation, that you do not
see me in the Park, where I should have to
ride up and down that ghastly Row, and talk
nonsense to the fribbles and the fools I meet
there. It is precisely in search of the relaxation you speak of that I ride out to the north-

west or the south-east; it little matters to me where, so long as I can find fresh air and green trees, and the absence of my fellow-creatures.'

'You are polite, by Jove,' said his friend with a laugh, 'considering that I have just joined you.'

'O, I don't mean you, Lingard,' said Mr. Wetter; 'my ride is over for the day. When I reach the turnpike yonder, I look upon myself as within the confines of civilisation, and behave myself accordingly.'

'You certainly are a very extraordinary fellow,' said Mr. Lingard, who was one of those gushing creatures whom nothing could silence. 'They were talking of you only yesterday at the Darnley Club.'

'Indeed,' said Wetter, without betraying the slightest interest in his manner; 'and what were they pleased to say of me?'

'They were saying what a wonderful fellow you were, considering that whereas, three years ago, you had scarcely been heard of in London, you had made such a fortune and held such a leading position.'

'Yes,' said Mr. Wetter, with a pleasant smile; 'they said that, did they?'

'What Mr. Sleiner wondered was, that you did not get yourself made a baronet, like those other fellows.'

'Ah, that was Sleiner,' said Mr. Wetter, still with his smile.

'And Mopkinson said you would not care about that. He believed you intended to marry a woman of high family.'

'Ah, that was Mopkinson,' said Mr. Wetter, still smiling.

'Podlinbury said marriage was not in your way at all, and then they all laughed.'

'Did Podlinbury say that?' said Mr. Wetter, grinning from ear to ear. 'Now I really cannot conceive what should have made them all laugh.'

'I cannot imagine myself,' said Mr. Lingard, 'and I told them so, and then they all roared worse than ever.'

'Let me make amends for your having been laughed at on my account, my dear Lingard, by asking you to dinner. Come and dine with me at the club to-night. We shall have time to wash our hands and to get to table by half-past eight.'

'No, not to-night, thanks,' said Mr. Lingard; 'I am engaged, and I must push on, by the way, for I dine at eight. Shall we meet on Friday?'

'Friday! Where?'

'At the house of one of your City magnates. You know him, I suppose—Mr. Calverley?'

'Mr. Calverley! Is there a dinner at his house in Great Walpole-street on Friday?'

'O, yes,' said Mr. Lingard ; 'a grand spread, I should imagine. A case of fortnight's invitation. Sorry you are not going ; thought I should be sure to meet you there. Ta, ta!' And the young man kissed his hand in adieu and cantered away.

' That's a delightful young creature,' said Mr. Wetter to himself, as he watched his friend's departing figure. ' If there were only a few more like him in the City, it would not take me long to complete that fortune which

I am piling together. With what frankness
and innocence he repeats all that is said about
one by one's friends; and how refreshingly
he confides to one everything concerning himself, even to his dinner-engagements. By the
way, that reminds me of that dinner-party at
Calverley's on Friday. At that dinner-party
Calverley will necessarily be present. Friday
would not be a bad day, therefore, for me to
ride up again to Hendon, make some excuse
for calling at the nest, and see if I can manage
to get a sight of the bird. I will make a mem.
to that effect when I go in.'

'The world was right in declaring Mr.
Wetter to be a very wealthy man. He was
the second partner in, and English representative of, the great Vienna banking-house of
Wetter and Stutterheim, with branches in
Paris, London, Frankfort, and New York.
He came to London quite unknown, save to a
few of his countrymen; but he was speedily
spoken of as a man of immense capacity, and
as a financier of the first rank. Perfectly
steady-going people were Wetter and Stutter-

heim, doing a straight-forward banking and agency business, with its quintupled operations, based upon the principles laid down by the old house of Krebs et Cie. to whom they had succeeded. Wetter and Stutterheim smiled with scorn at the wonderful schemes which were daily brought forward upon the Stock Exchange, and at the status and supposed success of the persons by whom they were 'promoted' and 'financiered.' They knew well enough how those matters were worked, and knew, too, what was generally the fate of those involved in them. Wetter and Stutterheim were quite content with the state of their balance on the thirty-first of every December, and content with the status which they occupied in the eyes of the chief merchant princes of the various cities where their banking business was carried on.

Mr. Stutterheim managed the parent house in Vienna—the parent house, however, did not do a fourth of the business transacted by its London offspring—and only came to London once or twice a year. He was an elderly

man, steady and responsible, but did not com-
bine dash and energy with his more solid business qualifications as did Mr. Henrich Wetter,
the head of the London house.

Mr. Wetter lived in pleasant rooms in
South Audley-street; that is to say, he slept
in them, and drank a hurried cup of coffee
there in the morning when he did not breakfast at his club; but in general he followed
the continental fashion, and took his first meal
at about twelve o'clock in his private room
at the bank, after he had gone through, and
given his instructions upon, the morning's
letters. He returned to his lodging to dress
for dinner; he dressed always punctiliously,
whether he dined in society or by himself at
the club, and was seldom out of his bed after
midnight. A man whom no one could accuse
of any positive excess, who lived strictly within
his means, and who was never seen in any dis-
reputable company; yet a man at the mention
of whose name in certain society there went
round winks and shoulder-shrugs, and men
hinted 'that they could, and if they would,' &c.

Henrich Wetter did not pay much attention to these hints, or rather to the men from whom they came. They were not the style of men whose good or bad words were likely to have the smallest influence on his career; his position was far too secure to be affected by anything they might say.

By anything any one might say, for the matter of that. He was full of that thought as he rode home after leaving Mr. Lingard. He had played his cards well in his wildest dreams, but he had never hoped to climb to the height at which he had actually arrived. Wealth? He did not spend a fifth part of his income. His old mother had her villa at Kreuznech, where she lived with his sister Lisbett, while Ernestine was married to Dom-hardt, who, thanks to him and his lent capital, was doing so well as a wine-grower at Hoch-heim. Fritz seemed to have settled down at last, and to be establishing for himself a bu-siness as Domhardt's agent in Melbourne. There was no one else of his own blood to support. There were others who had claims

on him, but those claims were allowed and
provided for, and there was still more money
than he knew with what to do. Position?
Not much doubt about that. Men of the
highest rank in the City allowed his status
to be equal to their own; and as to his own
house, the other partners had practically acknowledged that he was its backbone and
their superior. For instance, when there was
that question, a month ago, about the manner
in which their New York agency was conducted, to whom did they refer but to him?
If Rufus P. Clamborough had turned out a
rogue, he would have had to go out, he thought,
to settle the business there. Yes, to have the
money and to have the position were both
pleasant things. To gain them he sacrificed
nearly all his life, and certainly he needed
some little recreation. What a wonderful
pretty girl that was at Rose Cottage, and how
extraordinary that he should have discovered
old John Calverley there! How lucky, too,
that he should have met Lingard! The great
dinner-party in Great Walpole-street was to

be on Friday. On Friday, then, he would ride out by Hendon once again.

But Mr. Wetter did not ride out to Hendon on Friday, as he intended. On that Friday night he slept at the Adelphi Hotel, Liverpool, going off in the tender at 8.30 the next morning to the Cunard steamer China, lying in the Mersey, and not returning to England for nearly six months. On the evening of his meeting Mr. Lingard, on his arrival at South Audley-street, he found a telegram which had been forwarded to him from the City, informing him that Rufus P. Clamborough had by no means come out as rightly as was anticipated, and that it was imperative that some one should go out at once and look after the New York agency. Mr. Wetter was, above all things, a man of business, and he knew that that some one was himself, so he packed his portmanteau and went off. And finding an immense deal of business to be done, and life in New York city anything but disagreeable, he remained there until he had placed the affairs of Stutterheim and Wetter on a satisfactory footing, and then, and not till then, he took ship and came home.

Three weeks after Mr. Wetter's return to England, Miss M'Craw saw him once again in the Hendon lane. It was spring time when she had last seen him, but now it was deep autumn, and the dead leaves were whirling through the air, and being gathered into heaps by the old men employed as scavengers by the parish. Miss M'Craw was alone in her little parlour, and had no friends to share her watch. Nevertheless, she did not allow her attention to be diverted from Mr. Wetter for an instant. She saw him ride up, followed by his groom, but instead of gazing over the hedge he rode straight to the front gate, over which appeared a painted board announcing the house as to let, and referring possible inquirers to the village agent and to the auctioneers in London.

Miss M'Craw saw Mr. Wetter yield up his horse to his groom, dismount, ring the bell, and pass out of her sight up the garden. When he reached the door it was already opened by the servant, who was standing there, to whom he intimated his desire to see the house. The girl asked him into the dining-room, and withdrew. Five minutes afterwards the door opened, and Pauline entered the room. The sun had set about five minutes previously, and there was but little daylight left, so little that Mr. Wetter, glancing at the new comer, thought he must have been deceived, and made a step forward, staring hard at her.

There was something in the movement which put Pauline on her mettle instantly.

'May I ask your business?' said she, in a hard, dry tone.

'The voice, the accent—no doubt about it now,' said Mr. Wetter to himself. Then he said aloud, 'I see this house is to let; I ask to be permitted to look over it.'

'The house cannot be seen without a card from the agent in the village, Mr. Bowles,' said Pauline, in her former tone. 'And I may as well remark that Mr. Bowles will not give a card to every one. He will expect a reference.'

'I shall be very happy to give him one,' said Mr. Wetter, with a sardonic smile. 'My name is Henrich Wetter, formerly clerk to Monsieur Krebs, the banker, of Marseilles; and I shall be happy to refer him to an old acquaintance of mine, Madame Pauline Lunelle, dame du comptoir at the Restaurant du Midi in that city.'

CHAPTER II.

DULY PRESENTED.

THE words of recognition uttered by Mr.
Wetter filled Pauline with the utmost consternation. What! was this elegant gentleman, who stood before her with an amused
smile on his handsome face, the same Henrich
Wetter, the blonde and lymphatic clerk to
Monsieur Krebs?

As she stared at him the features grew
familiar to her, and she saw that he was prac-
tising no deception. Henrich Wetter! He
knew all about her former life, then, and, if
he chose, could, with a word, destroy the neat
fabric of invention which she had so carefully
raised. He could tell any one, whose interest
it would be to know it, all about her position
at the Restaurant du Midi, all about her marriage with Tom Durham, perhaps even some

of the particulars of her life since her marriage. It would be most advisable to keep
on good terms with a man of so much knowledge. So, all these thoughts having flashed
instantaneously through Pauline's mind, she
turned to her companion with a look in
which astonishment and delight were admirably blended, and stretched out her hand in
the frankest and friendliest manner.

'You must not be astonished at my not
recognising you, Monsieur Wetter,' she said;
'it is long since we met, and in the interval
you are so much changed, and, if I may say
it, so much improved.'

Mr. Wetter smiled blandly and easily.

'And you, Pauline—' he said.

Pauline started as he pronounced the name.
Her husband was the only man who had so
addressed her since the old days at Marseilles,
and, of course, she had not heard it since his
death.

'And you, Pauline,' he continued, 'how
well and handsome you look! How prosperous you seem!'

'Do I, Monsieur Wetter?' she said, with a characteristic shoulder-shrug, 'do I? It must be, then, because I have a light heart and a strong will of my own; for I have not been without my troubles, and heavy ones too. However, these are matters in which you could feel no possible interest, and with which I will not pretend to worry you.'

'I feel no interest in what concerns you?' said Mr. Wetter, with elevated eyebrows. 'Why, what do you imagine brought me to this house?'

'Information that the house was to let, and a desire to see if it would suit your purpose.'

'Suit my purpose?' repeated Mr. Wetter, with a half-sneering laugh. 'And what do you imagine my purpose to be, Pauline? I am a man of action and of business. It would not suit me to drone away my life in this rural solitude; my home must be in London, where my time is spent.'

'Perhaps you came to look at the house for a friend?' said Pauline.

'Wrong again,' he cried; 'my friends are
like myself, men to whom this house, from its
situation, would be absolutely useless. Now,
what do you say if I were to tell you,' he said,
leaning on the table, and bending towards her
as he spoke, 'that the memory of the old days
has never passed away from my mind, of the
old days when Adolphe de Noailles and I ran
neck and neck for the hand of the prettiest
girl in Marseilles, and when we were both
beaten by the English escroc who took her
away from us?'

'Monsieur Wetter,' said Pauline, holding
up her hand, 'he was my husband.'

'You are right in saying *was*, Pauline;
for he is dead, and you are free. You see,'
he added, in amusement at the amazed expression on her face, 'I keep myself tolerably
well informed as to the movements of those
in whom I have at any time taken an interest.'

'And by your—your inquiries you learned
that I was here?' she asked.

'No,' he replied; 'truth to tell, that was

entirely accidental. I have only just returned from America, and as I was riding by here a few days ago I thought I perceived you at the window. At first I doubted the evidence of my senses, and even when I had satisfied myself, I was so completely upset that I could not attempt to come in. I went home meditating on what I had seen, and determining to come out again on the first opportunity. As I rode out to-day I was debating within myself what excuse I could possibly offer for intruding upon you without announcing myself, as I wished to ascertain whether you would recognise me, when the board at the gate, advertising the house to let, fortunately afforded me the necessary excuse; and how the rest of the little comedy was played out you are aware.'

Pauline looked at him earnestly for some moments, as though desirous of ascertaining whether he had correctly stated the motive by which he professed himself animated. The result of her survey seemed to be satisfactory, for she said to him:

'I need scarcely tell you, Monsieur Wetter, that I am much flattered by what you have said, or that I am very much pleased to see you again.'

'And on my part,' said he, taking her hand and gallantly raising it to his lips, 'I need scarcely say that the pleasure is mutual. I hope I shall often be allowed to visit you in this house?'

'Not in this house,' said Pauline. 'You forget the board at the gate. There is no deception about that. This house is veritably to let, and we are about to leave it as soon as possible.'

'Why?' said Mr. Wetter, interrogatively.

'Why?' interrupted Pauline. 'I forgot to mention that I am not here alone, and that this is not my house. There is another lady with me.'

'O, indeed; another lady?' said Wetter, brightening. 'And who may she be?'

The change in his manner was not lost upon Pauline.

'She is a lady who has just lost her hus-

band,' said she coldly. 'Her bereavement is
so recent, and she feels it so acutely, that she
will see no one, nor will she remain in this
house where she lived with him.'

'Poor creature!' said Mr. Wetter, shaking
his head. 'No one with any feeling would
desire to intrude upon her. And will you
continue to live with her when she moves to
a new abode?'

'I shall,' said Pauline, still coldly. 'She
depends upon me greatly for advice and assistance.'

'And that new abode will be—?' he asked
insinuatingly.

'I cannot say at present,' she replied; 'nothing is decided. We have, indeed, scarcely
had time to look out.'

'You will let me know when you have
fixed upon a spot, will you not?' he said. 'I
am going out of town for some shooting, but
I shall not be more than a month away; and
I should like to carry with me the thought
that the renewal of an acquaintance so dear to
me is not a mere temporary measure.'

His manner was as earnest and as gallant as before, and his eyes were as expressive as his words; but Pauline still answered him coldly: 'You shall have a line from me stating where I have pitched my tent if you will tell me where to send it.'

He gave her his address in South Audley-street; and as there was nothing more to be done, rose and took his leave. As he bade her adieu he once more raised her hand to his lips, and reiterated his hope of speedily hearing from her.

Pauline walked to the window, and looked out after him. She heard his retreating footsteps, but it was too dark to see his figure. Then, as she turned away, her face was set and rigid, and she muttered to herself, 'Connu, monsieur! connu! Though I was very nearly being taken in by your bland manner and the softly sympathetic voice in which you spoke of those old memories. If it had not been for that sly look at the corner of your eyes, which you always had, and which I recognised at once when you spoke of the subject in which

you were really interested, I might have imagined that it was on my account you had
taken the trouble to ride out here, that to
renew your friendship with me was the one
great wish of your life. It is all plain to me
now. He has seen Alice, and is dying for an
introduction to her. He tried to avail himself
of the circumstance of the house being to let,
was baffled for the moment when he recognised me, but had sufficient mother - wit to
enable him to concoct a story by which I was
so nearly taken in. I, with whom all vanity
ought to have died out years ago, whose knowledge of the world ought to have led me at
once to suspect the hollowness of Monsieur
Wetter's profession!

'He wants an introduction to Alice, that
is it undoubtedly; and for what end? He is
amazingly changed, this garçon! He is no
longer lymphatic, romantic in the highest
degree, mawkish, or Teutonic; he rides on
horseback, and affects the air of conquest.
There is about him a smack of the gallant, of
the coureur des dames. He is a man whom

Alice would not like, but still it is as well that
she did not see him at this particular time.
He is going out of town, he said; and when
he comes back we shall have moved into another house, our change of address will not be
recorded in the fashionable newspapers, and,
as I shall take care that it is not sent to
Monsieur Wetter at South Audley-street, it is
probable that he will know nothing about it.
And so,' she added, drawing down the blinds
as she heard Alice's footsteps on the stairs,
'bon soir, Monsieur Wetter.'

And for his own part, Mr. Wetter, as he
rode back to London, was full of his reflections.

'What a wonderful thing,' he thought to
himself, ' that I should have come across Pauline Lunelle in that house, and how lucky that
I recognised her instantly, and was enabled,
by playing upon her vanity, to put her off the
scent of the real motive of my visit, and induce her to believe that I had come to see her!
Let me see; all the points of the story seem to
fit and dovetail together admirably. Pauline

spoke of her companion as a widow—yes,
that's right. I saw the notice of John Calverley's death just before I left New York. She
said too, that her husband, the escroc, was
dead—that also is right. I recollect reading
the story of his having been drowned some
time ago. Ay, and now I remember that it
spoke of him, Mr. Durham, as having been in
the employ of Messrs. Calverley. This would
account for Pauline's presence in that house,
and her intended connexion with that pretty
girl. So far so good; je prend mon bien où
je le trouve; and I think in the present instance I shall not have far to look for it.
Mademoiselle Pauline Lunelle, ex-dame du
comptoir, will be too much frightened at the
idea of having the story of her own youth set
before her friends to refuse to aid me in any
way that I may wish.'

It was curious to note how Alice had
accepted Pauline's companionship as a matter
of course, and how she seemed to cling to the
Frenchwoman for society in that dark period
of her life. When Martin Gurwood visited her

soon after her convalescence, he conducted himself, under Humphrey Statham's directions, with all the formality and authority of a duly appointed guardian, and as such Alice received him. Amongst the business matters which were discussed between them, the appointment of Pauline to her new charge naturally held a prominent place. Martin imagined that he might have had some difficulty in bringing Alice to his views; but Pauline had already made herself so useful and agreeable to the broken-hearted girl, relieving her of all trouble, and showing, without the least ostentation, that she thoroughly sympathised with her grief, that Alice was only too glad to learn that, for some time at least, her home was to be shared by a person so capable of nuderstanding her position and ministering to her wants. And Martin Gurwood himself did not fail to notice the alteration in Madame Du Tertre's demeanour, the gentleness of her manner towards Alice, the delicacy with which she warded off any chance allusion that might have pained her, and the eagerness and anxiety she exhibited to do her service. Martin mentioned these facts to Humphrey Statham, who received the communication in the most matter-of-fact manner, and said something to the effect ' that he was glad to hear that the Frenchwoman was earning her money;' which Martin, who was essentially soft-hearted, and who surrounded everything connected with Alice with a halo of romance, thought rather a brutal speech.

Uncaring in most matters, assenting not languidly—for, poor child, she strove to feign an interest which she did not feel, and failed most signally in the attempt—to all that was proposed to her, Alice had yet one real anxiety, and that was to get away as quickly as possible from Rose Cottage. The place had become hateful to her; everywhere, in the house, in the garden, there was something to remind her of the kind old man who had loved her so, and whom she had lost for ever. She wanted to be rid of it all, not merely the house, but the furniture, with its haunting memories; and most fortunately there arrived one day

an American gentleman, whose business compelled him to dwell in England for a few
years, during which period he must be two or
three times a week in London, and who was
so charmed with the cottage and its contents
that he took the lease of the first, and pur-
chased the second 'right away,' as he expressed
it, at the price demanded for it.

Then what was to be done, and where were
they to go to? Alice had expressed a decided
objection to the country; and it was accordingly decided that the new residence must be
either in London itself, or in some immediate
suburb. So advertisements in the newspapers
were eagerly consulted, and likely house-agents
were daily besieged by Martin Gurwood and
Statham; until one day, just before the time
when it was necessary that Rose Cottage should
be given up, the latter gentleman brought word
that he had seen what he thought would be a
suitable house. It was the corner house in
a new street of the old village of Chelsea,
and from its side-window one had a pleasant
glimpse of the river and the green fields and

waving trees on the farther shore. A neat, unpretending, comfortable little house, neatly and comfortably furnished with the money derived from the sale of the contents of Rose Cottage, suited to Alice's means, where she could live peaceably, exciting less curiosity, perhaps, than in a more retired spot. From nine in the morning till five in the evening scarcely a man, save the tradespeople of the neighbourhood, were seen in the street, but there were plenty of lady-like women and children, with their nursemaids, passing to and fro, and to many of these Alice became speedily known as 'the pretty, delicate-looking lady at number nine.' All attempts at visiting were declined on the score of Mrs. Claxton's ill health, and the necessity for her maintaining perfect quietude. But Pauline had a bowing acquaintance with several of the neighbours, and was highly popular among the children.

In the early days of their tenancy Martin Gurwood was a daily visitor; and the intense respectability of his appearance did much to

influence the neighbours in Alice's favour.
On several occasions he was accompanied by
Humphrey Statham; and when, after a short
time, Martin had to return to his vicarage at
Lullington, Mr. Statham came up once or
twice a week and took tea with the ladies,
both of whom were impressed with his gentlemanly bearing, his modesty, and his practical
good sense. They had no other visitors; so
it was not astonishing that one evening, when
their only servant was out, and Alice, feeling
somewhat fatigued, was lying down in her bed-
room, Pauline, seated at the window in the
dusk, seeing a tall bearded gentleman making
for the house, imagined him to be Humphrey
Statham, and went herself to let him in. But
her surprise was only equalled by her dismay
when, on looking up, she found herself con-
fronted by Henrich Wetter.

For an instant she stood in the doorway
irresolute, but as the new-comer politely but
firmly pressed into the passage, she felt constrained to ask him to walk into the parlour,
and followed him there.

'Now really I am obliged to call this an exhibition of very bad manners, my dear Madame Durham.'

'For Heaven's sake!' cried Pauline, interrupting him; 'I am Madame Du Tertre!'

'By all means,' said Mr. Wetter pleasantly; 'my dear Madame Du Tertre, then. In the first place you failed in fulfilling your agreeable promise to send me your new address; and when, with infinite labour and pains, I have discovered it, you seem as though you were inclined to close your door against me.'

'It was a mistake,' murmured Pauline; 'I did not recognise you in the darkness; I took you for some one else.'

'Took me for some one else!' he repeated with a laugh. 'Mistook me for one of those gay gallants who besiege your door, and who is out of favour for the time!'

The levity of his tone grated on Pauline's ear. 'You are labouring under a mistake, Monsieur Wetter,' she said. 'We, that is to say I, have but few friends, and certainly no acquaintances of the kind you indicate.'

'Do you look upon me as one of those acquaintances of the kind I indicate,' said Mr. Wetter, lying lazily back in his chair and smiling placidly at her, 'and that it is for that reason you have failed in sending me your address?'

'It is so long since we knew anything of each other, that I should be uncertain in what category of my acquaintance to class you, Monsieur Wetter,' said Pauline, becoming desperately annoyed at his self-sufficiency and nonchalance. 'The reason that you did not receive my address was, that I had lost yours, and I did not know where to write to you.'

'Quite a sufficient excuse,' he said, 'and no more need be said about the matter, unless I call your attention to the fact, that despite your negligence, I have discovered you, and have brought to that discovery an amount of perseverance and skill which would—'

'Which would have been better employed in a worthier cause,' said Pauline, interrupting him.

'A worthier cause !' said Mr. Wetter. 'How could that be ? There can be nothing better than the restoration of an old friendship, unless,' he added, half under his breath, 'unless it be the commencement of a new one.'

His tone was so eminently provoking, that despite her better reason, Pauline suffered herself to be betrayed into an expression of annoyance.

' It is not the restoration of an old friendship that brings you here, Monsieur Wetter,' she said, settling herself stiffly, and glaring at him. ' Your memory, of which you prate, cannot serve you very well if you take me for a fool.'

' My dear Mademoiselle Lunelle, Madame Durham, Madame—I beg your pardon, I have forgotten the most recent appellation—you do me a serious injustice in imagining that I take you for anything of the kind. The way in which you managed your affairs at Marseilles would have prevented my having any such ideas.'

'And yet you think to blind and hoodwink me by pretending that you are very glad to see me.'

'I am very glad to see you,' said Mr. Wetter, smiling; 'I can give you my word of honour of that.'

'But why—why, I ask?' said Pauline vehemently.

'Because I think you can be of use to me,' said Mr. Wetter, bending forward, and bringing his hand down with force upon the table. 'It is well to be explicit about that.'

'Of use to you,' said Pauline. 'In what way?'

'By introducing me to the lady who was living with you out in that country place where I last had the pleasure of seeing you, who is now living with you in this house. I have taken a fancy to her, and desire the pleasure of making her acquaintance.'

'Monsieur, que d'honneur!' exclaimed Pauline, with curling lip, and making him a mock obeisance. 'How flattered she ought to be at this proof of your esteem!'

'Don't be satirical, Mademoiselle Lunelle
—it is best to stick to the name which I know
once to have been really yours,' said Mr.
Wetter, with a certain amount of savageness;
'don't be satirical; it does not become you,
and it offends me.'

'Offends!' cried Pauline.

'Offends,' repeated Mr. Wetter. 'I have
asked you to do nothing extraordinary, nothing but what any gentleman might ask of
any lady.'

'And suppose I were to refuse—suppose I
were to decide from pique, jealousy, or whatever other motive you may choose to accredit
me with, that it was inexpedient for me to
present you to my friend—what then?'

'Then,' said Mr. Wetter, with smiling lips,
but with an unpleasant look in his eyes, 'I
should be forced to present myself. I have
made up my mind to make this lady's acquaintance, and it's a characteristic of mine,
that I invariably carry out what I once under-
take, and in making her acquaintance, I should
have occasion to inquire how much she knew

of the character and antecedents of the person
who was domesticated with her.'

'You threaten ?' cried Pauline.

'Everything,' said Mr. Wetter, again bringing his hand down upon the table. 'And I
not merely threaten, but I execute! Your
position at Marseilles, the name and social
status of your husband, and the circumstances
under which you married him,—all these will
be news I should think to Mrs.— by the way
you have not told me how the lady calls herself.'

While he had been speaking Pauline's head
had fallen upon her breast. She raised it now
but a very little as she said, 'Her name is
Claxton; I will present you to her whenever
you choose.'

'Of course you will,' said Mr. Wetter, gaily
touching her hand with the back of his. 'And
there is no time like the present for such a
pleasurable interview. She is in the house, I
suppose.'

'She is,' said Pauline.

'Very well, then; introduce me at once.

By the way, it will be advisable perhaps to say that I am your cousin, or something of that sort. We are both foreigners, you know, and English people are not clever in distinguishing between Germans and French either in name or accent.'

Pauline bowed her head and left the room. Five minutes afterwards she returned, bringing Alice with her. Her lips trembled, and her face was deadly pale, as she said, 'My dear, permit me to present to you my cousin, Monsieur Henrich Wetter.'

CHAPTER III.

Mr. Henrich Wetter did not remain long
in Pollington-terrace on the day of his introduction to Mrs. Claxton. He saw at once
that Mrs. Claxton was delicate and out of
health, and he was far too clever a man of
the world to let the occasion of his first visit
be remembered by her as one when she was
bored or wearied. While he remained, he
discussed pleasantly enough those agreeable
nothings, which make up the conversation
of society, in a soft mellifluous voice, and
exhibited an amount of deference to both
ladies.

On taking his leave, Mr. Wetter rather
thought that he had created a favourable
impression upon Alice, while Pauline thought
just the contrary. But the fact was that

Alice was not impressed much either one
way or the other. The man was nothing to
her; no man was anything to her now, or
ever would be again, she thought; but she
supposed he was gentlemanly, and she knew
he was Madame Du Tertre's cousin, and she
was grateful for the kindness which Madame
Du Tertre had shown to her. So when Mr.
Wetter rose to depart, Alice feebly put out
her little hand to him, and expressed a hope
that he would come again to see his cousin.
And Mr. Wetter bowed over her hand, and
much to Pauline's disgust declared he should
have much pleasure in taking Mrs. Claxton
at her word. His farewell to Pauline was
not less ceremonious, though he could scarcely
resist grinning at her when Mrs. Claxton's
back was turned. And so he went his way.

It accorded well with Pauline's notions
that immediately after Mr. Wetter's departure,
Alice should complain of fatigue, and should
intimate her intention of retiring into her
own room; for the fact was that she herself
was somewhat dazed and disturbed by the

occurrences of the day, and was longing for an opportunity of being alone and thinking them out at her leisure.

So, as soon as she had the room to herself, Pauline reduced the light of the lamp and turned the key in the door—not that she expected any intrusion, it was merely done out of habit—and then pushing the chairs and the table aside, made a clear path for herself in front of the fire, and commenced walking up and down it steadily. Pauline Lunelle! She had not heard the name for years. What scornful emphasis that man laid on it as he pronounced it! How he had boasted of his money and position! With what dire vengeance had he threatened her if she refused to aid him in his schemes! Of what those schemes were he had given her no idea, but they were pretty nearly certain to be bad and vicious. She recollected the opinion she had had of Henrich Wetter in the old days at Marseilles, and it was not a flattering one. People considered him an eligible match, and were greatly astonished when she had refused his hand; she, a poor dame du comptoir, to give up the opportunity of an alliance with such a rising man! But she had her feeling about it then, and she had it now.

It was, then, as she suspected during their interview at Rose Cottage. Wetter had seen Alice, had been attracted by her beauty, and had found, as he imagined, in Pauline an instrument ready made to his hand to aid him in his purpose. That acquaintance with her past life gave him a firm hold upon her, of which he would not hesitate to avail himself. Was it necessary that she should be thus submissive, thus bound to do what she was bid, however repulsive it might be to her? There was nothing of actual guilt or shame in that past life which Monsieur Wetter could bring against her; she had been merry, light, and frivolous, as was usual with people of her class—ah, of her class—the sting was there! Would Martin Gurwood have suffered her to hold the position in that household? would he have trusted or borne

with her at all, had he known that in her
early days she had been the dame du comptoir at a restaurant in a French provincial
town?

How insultingly that man had spoken of
her dead husband! Her dead husband? Yes,
Tom Durham was dead! She had long since
ceased to have any doubt on that point.
There was no motive that she could divine
for his keeping himself in concealment, and
she had for some time been convinced that
all he had said to her was true, and that his
plan of action was genuine, but that he had
been drowned in attempting to carry it out.
Where was the anguish that six months ago
she would have experienced in acknowledg-
ing the truth of this conviction? Why does
the idea of Tom Durham's death now come
to her with an actual sense of relief? Throughout her life, Pauline, however false to others,
had been inexorably true to herself; and that
she now feels not merely relief but pleasure
in believing Tom Durham to be dead, she
frankly acknowledges.

Whence this apparently inexplicable alteration in her ideas? She must have been fond of Tom Durham; for had she not toiled for him and suffered for his sake? How is it, then, that she could bring herself to think of his death with something more than calmness? Because she loved another man, whom to win would be life, redemption, rehabilitation; to keep whom in ignorance of the contamination of the past she would do or suffer anything! There was but one way in which that past could be learned, and that was through Wetter. He alone held the key to that mystery, and to him, therefore, must the utmost court be paid—his will must be made her law. Stay, though! If Monsieur Wetter's projects are as base as she is half inclined to suspect them, by aiding them in ever so little, even by keeping silence about her suspicions, she betrays Martin's confidence and injures some of his best feelings!

What a terrible dilemma for her to be placed in! In that household where she has accepted a position of trust, and is accredited by Martin as Alice's guardian. In that position it was her duty to shield the young girl in every possible way, and not even to have permitted such a person as she believed Monsieur Wetter to be to have been introduced into the house. Being herself the actual means of introducing him, had she not virtually betrayed the trust reposed in her? and yet — and yet! Let her once set this man at defiance, 'and he would not scruple to utter words which would have the effect of exiling her from the house, and taking from her every chance of seeing the man for whom alone in the world she had a gentle feeling. A word from Wetter would be sufficient to annihilate the fairy palace of hope which during the last few days she had been building, and to send her forth a greater outcast than ever upon the world!

No, that could not be expected of her; it would be too much! The glimpse of happiness which she had recently enjoyed, unsubstantial though it was—a mere figment of her

own brain, a dream, a delusion—had yet so
far impressed her, that she could not willingly
bring herself to part with it; nor, as she felt
after more mature reflection, was there any
necessity for her so doing. She might safely
temporise; the occasion when she would be
called upon to act decisively was not immi-
nent; the performers were only just placed
en scène, and there could be no possible
chance of a catastrophe for some time to
come. There was very little chance that
Alice Claxton, modest and retiring, filled with
the memories of her 'dear old John,' to whom
she was always referring, would be disposed
to accept the proferred attention of such a
man as Monsieur Wetter. Whether Monsieur
Wetter succeeded or not with Alice would
entirely depend upon himself. He could not
possibly know anything of her former life,
and could therefore bring no undue influence
to bear in his favour; and Pauline thought,
even suppose, as was most likely, that Alice
repulsed him, he could not turn round upon
her. She had done her best; she had given

him the introduction he required; and if he
did not prosper in his suit no blame could
be attached to her.   Matters must remain so,
she thought, and she would wait the result
with patience.

And Martin Gurwood, the man for whom
alone in the world she had a gentle feeling,
the man whom she loved — yes, whom she
loved! She was not ashamed, but rather
proud to acknowledge it to herself; the man
with the shy retiring manner, the delicate
appearance, the soft voice, so different from
all the other men with whom her lot in life
had thrown her—the very atmosphere seemed
to change as she thought of him. How well
she recollected her first introduction to him
in the grim house in Great Walpole-street,
and the distrust, almost amounting to dislike,
with which she had regarded him! She had
intended pitting herself against him then;
she would now be only too delighted for the
opportunity of showing him how faithfully
she could serve him. Distrust! Ay, she remembered the suspicion she had entertained,

that there was a secret on his mind which he kept hidden from the world. She thought so still. It pleased her to think so; for in her, with all her realism and practical business purpose, there was a strong dash of superstition and imagination, and that unconscious link between them, the fact that they each had something to conceal, seemed to afford her ground for hope.

Yes, her position towards Martin, though not quite what she might have desired, was by no means a bad one. He had had to trust her, he had had to acknowledge her intellectual superiority; he, a lonely man gradually growing accustomed to women's society. He hated it at first, but now he liked it; missed it when he was forced to absent himself: she had heard him say as much. She seated herself where Alice had previously sat, and leaned her arm upon the table, supporting her chin with her hand. Might not he, she thought, might not he come to care for her, to love her—well enough? That would be all she could expect, all she could hope—well enough!

A few years ago she would have scorned the idea; even up to within the last few weeks she would not have accepted any half-hearted affection. A passionate domineering woman, with the hot southern blood running in her veins, unaccustomed, in that way at all events, to be checked or stayed, she must have had all or none. But now what a difference! Her love was now tempered by discretion, her common sense was allowed its due influence; and she was too wise, and in her inmost heart too sad, to expect a passionate attachment from the man whom she had set up as her idol. In the new-born humility which has come from this true love she will be satisfied to give that, and to take in return whatever he may have to offer her.

Married to Martin Gurwood, to the man whom she loved! Could such a lot possibly be in store for her? Could she dare to dream of such a haven of rest, after her life-long suffering with storms and trials? She was free now; of that there was no doubt; and he himself had acknowledged her energy and talent. The position which she then held was in the eyes of the world no doubt inferior to his — would be made more inferior if he accepted his share of the wealth which his mother had offered him. But he is not a man, unless she has read him wrongly, if he would otherwise marry her, to be deterred by social considerations; he is far beyond and above such mean and petty weaknesses. In her calm review of the position occupied by each of them, Pauline could see but one hopeless obstacle to her chance of inducing Martin Gurwood to marry her—that sole obstacle would be another affection. Another affection! Good Heaven!—Alice!

The suspicion went through her like a knife. Her brain seemed to reel, her arms dropped powerless on the table before her, and she sank back in the chair.

Alice! Let her send her thoughts back to the different occasions when she had seen Alice and Martin Gurwood together; let her dwell upon his tone and manner to the suffering girl, and the way in which she appeared

to be affected by them.   When did they first
meet? Not until comparatively recently, their
first interview being confessedly that which
she, unseen by them, had watched from the
narrow lane.   In the room at Pollington-
terrace, by the dull red light shed by the
expiring embers, Pauline saw it as plainly
as she had seen it in reality; the pitying
expression in Martin's face on that occasion,
the eyes full of sorrowful regard, the hands
that sought to raise her prostrate body, but
the motion of which was checked, as they
were folded across his breast.   He was not
in love with her then.   Pauline recollected
making the remark to herself at the time; but
since then what opportunities had they not
had of meeting, how constantly they had been
thrown together, and how, as proved by the
anxiety he had shown, and the trouble he
has taken on her behalf, his sympathy and
regard for the desolate girl had deepened and
increased!

Why should she doubt Martin Gurwood's
disinterestedness in this matter? Why should

she ascribe to him certain feelings by which
he may possibly never have been influenced?
He was a man of large heart and kindly sym-
pathies by nature, developed by his profession
and by his constant intercourse with the weak
and suffering. He would doubtless have befriended any woman in similar circumstances
who might have been brought under his notice. Befriended? Yes, but not, as Pauline honestly allowed to herself, in the same
way. His words would have been kind, and
his purse would have been open; but in all
his kindness to Alice there was a certain delicate consideration, which long before she even
thought it would trouble her, Pauline had
frequently remarked, and which she understood and appreciated all the better, perhaps,
because she had had no experience of any
such treatment in her life. That consideration spoke volumes as to the character of
Martin's feelings towards Alice, and Pauline's
heart sank within her as she thought of it.

Meanwhile she must suffer quietly, and
hope for the best; that was all left for her to

do. She was surprised at the calmness of her despair. In the old days her fiery jealousy of Tom Durham had leapt forward at the slightest provocation, rendering her oftentimes the laughing-stock of her husband and his ribald friends; now, when the first gathering of the suspicion crossed her mind that a man, far dearer to her than ever her husband had been, was in love with another woman, she accepted the position, not without dire suffering it is true, but with calmness and submission. It might not be the case, after all. From what little she had seen of Alice, Pauline scarcely suspected her of being the right woman to understand or appreciate Martin Gurwood. She had been accustomed to be petted and spoiled by an old man, who was her slave; she was not intended by nature to be much more than a spoilt child, a doll to be petted and played with, and the finer traits in Martin's character would be lost upon her. She was grateful to him as her benefactor, of course, but she had never exhibited any other feeling towards him, and Pauline did not think that she would allow her gratitude to have much influence over her future. Moreover—but, as Pauline knew perfectly well, little reliance was to be placed upon that—she professed herself inconsolable for her recent loss, and talked of perpetual widowhood as her only possible condition. So that Pauline thought that there were two chances, either of which would suit her—one that Alice would never marry again; the other that she might marry some one else in preference to Martin Gurwood.

It was growing late, and Pauline, wearied and exhausted, extinguished the lamp, and made the best of her way up the staircase in the dark. As she passed by the door of the room in which Alice slept, she thought she heard a stifled cry. She paused for an instant and listened; the cry was repeated, followed by a low moan. Alarmed at this, Pauline tried the door; it was unfastened, and yielded to her touch. Hurrying in, she found Alice sitting upright in her bed, her hair streaming

over her shoulders, and an expression of terror in her face.

'What on earth is the matter, poor child?'
cried Pauline, putting her arm round the girl,
and peering into the darkness. 'What has disturbed you in your sleep?'

'Nothing,' said Alice, placing her hand
upon her heart to still its beating; 'nothing
—at least, only a foolish fancy of my own.
Do not leave me,' she cried, as Pauline moved
away from her.

'I am not going to leave you, dear, be
sure of that,' said Pauline; 'I am only going
to get a light in order that I may be certain
where I am and what I am about. There,'
she said, as, after striking a match and light-
ing the gas, she returned to the bed. 'Now
you shall tell me what frightened you and
caused you to cry out so loudly.'

'Nothing but a dream,' said Alice. 'Is
it not ridiculous? But I could not help it, indeed I could not. I cried out involuntarily,
and had no idea of what had happened until
you entered the room.'

'And what was the dream that caused so great an effect?' asked Pauline, seating herself on the bed and taking Alice's trembling hand in hers.

'A very foolish one,' said Alice. 'I thought I was in the garden at Hendon, walking with dear old John and talking'— here her voice broke and the tears rolled down her face—'just as I used to talk to him, very stupidly no doubt, but he enjoyed it and so did I, and we liked it better, I think, because no one else understood it. We were crossing the lawn and going down towards the shrubbery, when a cold chilling wind seemed to blast across from the churchyard, and immediately afterwards a man rushed up—I could not see his face, for he kept it averted—and pulled John away from me and held him struggling in his arms. I could not tell now how it came about, but I found myself at the man's feet, imploring him to let John come to me. And the man told me to look up; and when I looked up John was gone, vanished, melted away! And when I

called after him, the man bade me hold my
peace, for that John was not what I had fan-
cied him to be, but, on the contrary, the worst
enemy I had ever had. Then the scene
changed, and I was in an hospital, or some
place of the sort, and long rows of white beds
and sick people lying in them. And in one
of them was John, so altered, so shrunken, pale,
and wobegone; and when he saw me he bowed
his head and lifted up his hands in supplication,
and all he said was, 'Forget! forget!' in such
a piteous tone; and I thought he did not know
me, and in my anguish I screamed out and
woke. Was it not a strange dream?'

'It was indeed,' said Pauline meditatively,
'but all dreams are—'

'Stay,' cried Alice, interrupting her; 'I
forgot to tell you that when I was struggling
with the man who kept me away from John,
I managed to look at his face, and it was the
face of the gentleman who came here last
night—your cousin, you know.'

'Ay,' said Pauline, looking at her quietly;
'there is nothing very strange in that. You

see so few people, that a fresh face is apt to be photographed on your mind, and thus my unfortunate cousin was turned into a monster in your dream. 'Do you think you are sufficiently composed now for me to leave you?'

'I'd rather you would stay a little longer, if you don't mind,' said Alice, laying her hand on her friend's. 'I know I'm very foolish, but I scarcely think I could get to sleep if I were left just now.'

'I am not at all sure,' said Pauline gently, 'that we have been right in keeping you so much secluded as we have done hitherto, and in declining the civilities and hospitalities which have been offered to us by all the people here about. I am afraid you are getting into rather a morbid state, Alice, and that this dream of yours is a proof of it.'

'I cannot bear the notion of seeing any one else,' said Alice.

'That is another proof of the morbid state to which I was referring,' said Pauline. 'You would very soon get over that, if the ice were once broken.'

'But surely we see enough people. Whenever he is in town, Mr. Gurwood comes to see us.'

Pauline's eyes were fixed full on Alice's face as she pronounced Martin's name, but they did not discover the slightest flush on the girl's cheeks, nor was there the least alteration in her tone.

'True,' said Pauline; 'and Mr. Statham comes to see us now and then.'

'O yes,' said Alice; 'I suppose whenever he has nothing more important to do; but Mr. Statham's time is valuable, and very much filled up, I have heard Mr. Gurwood say.'

'But even Mr. Statham and Mr. Gurwood,' said Pauline, forcing herself to smile, 'seen at long intervals, give us scarcely sufficient intercourse with the outer world to prevent our falling into what I call a perfectly morbid state; and on the next visit paid us by either of these gentlemen, I shall lay my ideas before them, and ask for authority to enlarge our circle. Now, dear, you are dropping with sleep, and all your terror seems thoroughly subsided. So, good-night. I will leave the light burning to drive away the evil dreams.'

As Pauline bent over Alice, the girl threw her arms round her friend's neck, and kissing her, thanked her warmly for her attention.

'A strange dream indeed!' said Pauline, as she walked slowly up the staircase to her own room. 'She was told that old John, as she calls him, instead of being what she always imagined, was really her worst enemy. And the man who told her so proved to be Henrich Wetter! A very strange dream indeed!'

CHAPTER IV.

WHAT has come over the ruling spirit of the offices in 'Change Alley? The partners in the great mercantile houses, whose shipbroking is there carried on, cannot understand it, and the men in the tall fluffy hats, the frock-coats, and the shepherd's plaid trousers, whom no one would suspect to be the captains of merchant vessels fully certificated, long-serviced, and ready to sail on any navigable water in the world, shrug their shoulders and mutter hoarsely to each other in the luncheon-room at Lloyd's, that 'something must be up with Mr. Statham.' The clerk who gives a maritime flavour to the office by wearing a pea-jacket, and who in default of any possible boating on the Thames or Serpentine is, during the winter, compelled to give vent to his nautical tendencies by vocal references at con- vivial supper-parties to his Lovely Nan, his Polly of Portsmouth, and other of the late Mr. Dibdin's creation, opines that there is a young woman in the case, and that his go- vernor has 'got smote.' Another of the clerks, an elderly man with a wooden leg and a mel- ancholy mind, who had more than once failed in business on his own account, began to hint in a mysterious manner that he foresaw bank- ruptcy impending, and that they should all have to look out for new situations before the spring. Mr. Collins, to whom all the querists addressed themselves, and at whom all the indirect hints were levelled, said nothing; he even refused to admit to the general public that there was any perceptible difference in Mr. Statham's manner. Only in conjugal confidence, as he smoked his after-supper pipe in the neatly-furnished parlour of his resi- dence in Balaclava-buildings East, Lower Clapham-road, he confessed to Mrs. C. that the chief had somehow lost his relish for business, and that he did not think Mr. S. was the man he had been.

If you had asked Humphrey Statham himself if there were any real foundation for these whispered hints and innuendoes, he would have laughed in your face. The forebodings of the melancholy man as to there being a decline in the business, he would have settled at once by a reference to Mr. Collins, who would have shown that never since he had been connected with the firm had their dealings been so large, and apparently so safe. As to Mr. Collins's connubial confidences, Humphrey Statham, if he had been made aware of them, would have said that they were equally ridiculous. Perhaps it was true that he did not care so much for business, was not so constantly at his desk, or such a dead hand at a bargain as he used to be; but it was natural enough that he should begin to slack off a little. He had been an idle dog in his early days, but ever since he settled down in the City, there were few men who had worked harder than he. The ten thousand pounds originally left him by his father he had more than trebled, and his personal disbursements certainly did not amount to more than six or seven hundred a year. Why should he slave away every moment of his life? Why should he be at the beck and call of every one who wanted his advice? They paid him for it, it was true. But he wanted something else besides payment now—amongst other things a certain amount of leisure for day-dreaming.

But what about the suggestion thrown out by the young gentleman of nautical tendency, —the suggestion involving the idea that his principal's absence of mind was referable to his thoughts being occupied with a young woman? Day-dreaming was surely in favour of the nautical young gentleman's theory. When Humphrey Statham, after giving strict orders that he was not to be disturbed, no matter who might want him, threw himself back in his chair, and burying his hands in his trousers' pockets, indulged in a long reverie, his thoughts reverted not to any busi-

ness transactions in which he might have
been engaged, but to the day when he first
went to Rose Cottage in the assumed character of a charity agent, and to the person with
whom he had the interview there. To Alice,
as he saw her then for the first time, with the
look of interest and anxiety in her pale wist-
ful face, with the tears standing in her large
hazel eyes, how graceful and elegant were all
her movements; in how tender and woman-
like a manner, regardless of her own trouble,
which, though not absolutely pronounced, she
felt to be impending, she sympathised with
him in the presumed object of his mission,
and promised him aid! Then she would rise
before his mind as he had seen her since,
chilled, almost numbed with sorrow, caring
for nothing, taking no interest in all that was
proposed to her, though always grateful and
recognisant. That look of hopeless, helpless
sorrow haunted Humphrey Statham's life.
Could it never be banished from her pale
face? Would her eyes never brighten again
with joy? The sorrowful look was a tribute

to one who had cruelly deceived her, who had merited her bitterest hatred for the manner in which he had treated her. A word, probably, would disperse those clouds of grief, would turn her from a weeping mourner to an outraged woman, would show her how terrible was her present position, and would probably render her wildly anxious to escape from it. But to speak that word to Alice, to acquaint her with John Calverley's crime, would be to point out to her her own degradation, to inflict upon her the sharpest wounds that brutality could devise, to uproot her faith in honesty and goodness, and to send her forth cowering before the world. The man who could do this would prove himself Alice Claxton's direst enemy; it was Humphrey Statham's hope to take rank as one of her dearest friends; and in this hope he suffered and was silent.

One of her dearest friends! Nothing more than that; he had never dared to hope that he should be anything more to her. She was likely to remain constant to the memory of

him whom she believed to have been her
husband, and no one who had her welfare at
heart would attempt to shake her in that con-
stancy. With the exception of the doctors,
indeed—who were not likely to trouble themselves—there was no one capable of giving
her the information so fatal to her peace of
mind, save the three tried friends who were
occupying themselves in watching over her.
Three tried friends? Yes, he thought he
might say that; for this Frenchwoman, whom
he had distrusted at first, seemed to be fulfilling her self-imposed duty with strictness
and singleness of purpose. Humphrey Statham was not a man likely to be imposed upon
by specious assurances, unless they were carried out by corresponding acts. When Martin Gurwood had made him acquainted with
Madame Du Tertre's proposal, he had agreed
to their acceptance *faut de mieux*, but only as
a temporary measure, and without any opinion
of their lasting qualities. However, since Pauline's association with the Pollington-terrace
household, he had carefully watched her, and

in spite as it were of himself, found himself
compelled to give her credit for unselfishness
and devotion to Alice's cause.   What might
be her motive, what the guiding-string of her
conduct, so long as it involved no danger to
Alice, was no concern of his.   Humphrey
Statham was too much a man of the world
to ascribe it entirely to the sense of wishing
to do her duty, or the gratification of an
overweening affection which she had taken
for the deserted girl.   He argued rather that
she herself had been the victim of some treachery or some disappointment in a degree similar
to that unconsciously suffered by Alice, and
that hence arose her sympathy for Mrs. Claxton, which, added to a dislike of the world,
had induced her to seek for the position of
Alice's companion.   But this idea Humphrey
Statham kept to himself, as being one rather
likely to frighten a man of Martin Gurwood's
simplicity, and to render him distrustful of
the woman who was really of very great use
and assistance to them.

Martin Gurwood had returned to Lulling-

ton, the affairs of the parish, as he stated, de-
manding his presence. Mrs. Calverley had de-
murred to his going, objecting to being left
alone. Martin had employed a curate during
his absence—she said, a man sufficiently quali-
fied to attend to the spiritual wants of the
farmers and persons of that kind, of whom the
parish was composed. But Martin thought
otherwise. He had been away quite long
enough, too long, he argued, for a proper dis-
charge of his duties. There might have been
many occasions on which the parishioners who
knew him well would have come to him for
assistance, while they would have been diffi-
dent in appealing in the same way to a
stranger. His mother retorted, although he
had not chosen to give her any explicit answer, she had made him an offer, the acceptance of which would remove him from Lullington, and then the farmers and labourers
would be compelled to pocket their pride—
if it could be called pride in such persons—
and either seek aid from the stranger or go
without. To which Martin had replied that

if he were to yield up his living, his successor, from the mere fact of his position, would not be a stranger, but would be the proper person to apply to. So Martin Gurwood had gone back to Lullington, leaving his mother highly incensed at his departure; and his friend, Humphrey Statham, had no one to talk to about Mrs. Claxton's beauty, patience, and forlorn condition.

It was on that account that Humphrey chiefly missed Martin. There was not much else in common between the two men; indeed, they had been acquainted for years without the acquaintance ripening into intimacy. From other persons and common friends Martin Gurwood had heard of Statham's cleverness and tact. On the occasion when he wanted a friend possessing such qualities he had sought out his old acquaintance, and found that rumour had not belied him. On his part Statham had to admire Martin Gurwood's simplicity and earnestness, and having the Hendon mystery to deal with, and a certain number of complications to steer through, the alliance between them was close and firm; but it had Alice Claxton and her welfare for its basis and its mainspring, and nothing more. Not that Humphrey Statham wanted anything more; he would have liked Martin Gurwood, however the connection with him had been brought about; but associated as it was with Alice, this most recent friendship had a most appreciable value in his eyes.

Martin was gone, and there was no longer any one to whom Humphrey Statham could indulge in confidential converse; so he took to reveries and day-dreaming, and thus gave rise to all the odd talk and speculation about him which was rife in the City. He had settled with Martin before he left, however, that he should go up, for a time at least, twice or thrice a week, perhaps, to Pollington-terrace to see how Mrs. Claxton was getting on, and write fully and candidly to Martin his impressions of what he saw; and for a time nothing could be pleasanter reading to one interested in the success of the new establish-

ment than these letters.   Alice seemed gradually to be gaining health and strength; and if
it could not be said that her spirits were
much improved, certainly in that way she
had suffered no relapse.   Madame Du Tertre
had come out infinitely more favourably than
Humphrey had expected of her.   She was
unwearying in her devotion to her young
friend, and her affectionate surveillance was
just exactly what was wanted to a young
woman in Alice's position.   The matter of
fending off neighbourly acquaintance, which
they had so much dreaded, had been admirably managed by Madame Du Tertre, who
had pleaded her young friend's recent bereavement and ill health as an excuse for their
not entering into society; while she had
rendered herself most popular by the courteous way in which she had made the announcement, by her kindness to the children,
and her *savoir faire* in general.   Martin Gurwood read all this with as great a pleasure as
Humphrey Statham wrote it.   All things
taken into consideration, nothing could be

progressing more favourably than the establishment in Pollington-terrace, built though
it was, as both men knew, upon a quicksand,
and liable to be engulfed at any moment.

These visits to Pollington - terrace were
the holidays in Humphrey Statham's life,
the days to be marked with a white stone,
to be dwelt upon both in anticipation and
recollection—days to be made much of, too,
and not to be carelessly enjoyed. Humphrey
Statham, since his early youth a prudent
man, was not inclined to be prodigal even
of such delights. Immediately after Martin's departure for the country he had been
a pretty constant visitor at Pollington-terrace, for the purpose, of course, of keeping
his friend properly posted up in all the move- -
ments of its denizens; but after a little he
thought it better to put in an appearance
less frequently, and he mortified himself
accordingly. One night, after a ten days'
interval, Humphrey thought he should be
justified in paying his respects to the lady,
and providing himself with subject-matter

for another letter to-morrow. Being, as has been said, a man of worldly wisdom, it was his habit to dismiss his cab at the end of the terrace, and proceed on foot to his destination, hansom cabs being looked upon by the staid neighbourhood as skittish vehicles, generally subversive of morals. When Humphrey reached the house, he saw upon the window-blind the unmistakable shadow of a man's head. Had Martin Gurwood suddenly returned to town? No — as the thought flashed across his mind, the head turned, showing him the profile, with a hook nose, and a flowing beard, with neither of which could the Vicar of Lullington be accredited. Humphrey Statham stopped short, scarcely daring to believe his senses. An instant's reflection convinced him of his folly. What rule was there forbidding these ladies to receive their acquaintances in their own house? Who was he to be startled at the unfamiliar silhouette on a window-blind? Why should such a sight cause him to stop suddenly in his walk, and set his heart thumping wildly

beneath his waistcoat? Martha, the little
maid-of-all-work was, at all events, not influenced by anything that had occurred. She
grinned when she saw Mr. Statham in her
usual friendly manner, and introduced him
into the parlour with her accustomed brisk-
ness of bearing.

Mrs. Claxton was there, so was Madame
Du Tertre, so was the original of the silhouette on the window-blind. A tall man this,
with a hooked nose, and a blonde silky beard,
and an easy pleasant manner, introduced as
Madame Du Tertre's cousin, Mr. Henrich
Wetter. A deuced sight too easy a manner,
thought Humphrey Statham to himself, as
he quietly remarked the way in which the
new - comer paid to Alice attentions, with
which no fault could be found, but were
unmistakably annoying to the looker-on, and
to that looker-on the behaviour of the strange
visitor was so ineffably, so gallingly patronising! Mr. Statham, did he catch the name
rightly? Was it Mr. Humphrey Statham of
Old 'Change? O, of course, then, he was

well known to everybody. They were neighbours in the City. He was very pleased to
make Mr. Statham's personal acquaintance.

'Confound his patronising airs!' thought
Humphrey Statham to himself. 'Who is
this German Jew — he is a German, undoubtedly, and probably a Jew — that he
should vaunt himself in this manner? And
how, in the name of fortune, did he find
himself in this house? Madame Du Tertre's
cousin, eh! This Wetter, if he be, as he
probably is, of the firm of Stutterheim and
Wetter, ought to have had sufficient respect for his family to have prevented his
cousin from taking the position occupied by
Madame Du Tertre. Bah! what nonsense
was he talking now? They had all reason
to be grateful that Madame Du Tertre was
in that position, and she was just the woman
who would keep her family in ignorance of
the circumstances under which she had
achieved it.

Exactly as he thought? The subsequent
conversation showed him how wrong he had

been. It turned accidentally enough upon
the number of foreigners domesticated in
England, a country where, as Mr. Wetter
remarked, one would have thought they would
have experienced more difficulty in making
themselves at home than in almost any other.

'Not that,' he said pleasantly—'not that
I have any reason to complain; but I am
now a naturalised Englishman, and all my
hopes and wishes—mere business hopes and
wishes—alas, Mrs. Claxton, I am a solitary
man, and have no other matters of interest
—are centred in this country. It was here,
though I confess with astonishment, that I
found my cousin, Madame Du Tertre, a per-
manent resident.'

'You were not aware then, Monsieur
Wetter,' said Statham, finding himself addressed, 'that your cousin was in England ?'

'Family differences, common to all na-
tions, had unfortunately separated us, and
for some years I had not heard of Pau—
Palmyre's movements.'

'You can easily understand, Mr. Statham,' said Pauline, speaking between her set teeth, 'that as my cousin's social position was superior to mine, I was averse to bringing myself under his notice.'

'We will say nothing about that,' said Mr. Wetter, with his pleasant smile. 'I think Mr. Statham will agree with me, that the social position which brings about a constant intercourse with Mrs. Claxton is one which any member of our sex would, to say the least of it, be proud.'

Humphrey Statham glanced round the circle as these words were uttered. Alice looked uncomfortable; Madame Du Tertre, savage and defiant; Mr. Wetter bland and self-possessed. There was silence for a few minutes. Then Pauline said: 'You have been a stranger for some time, Mr. Statham; we had been wondering what had become of you.'

'I am delighted to think that the void caused by my absence has been so agreeably filled,' said Humphrey Statham, with a bow towards Mr. Wetter. The next minute he cursed his folly for having made the speech, seeing by Wetter's look that he had thoroughly appreciated its origin.

'The regret of your absence indicated by Madame Du Tertre I fully share,' he said, with a polite smile. 'It is my great loss that I have not met you before in this charming society. At this dull season of the year, when every one is out of town, I need scarcely say what a godsend it has been to me to have been permitted to pass an evening occasionally with two such ladies; and the knowledge that I might have had the chance of an introduction to Mr. Humphrey Statham would have been, had it been needed, an additional inducement to drag me from my dreary solitude.'

That was an uncomfortable evening for all persons present. Even to Alice—dull, distrait, and occupied with her own sorrow— there was an evident incongruity in the meeting of the two men. Pauline was furious, partly at Wetter's cool treatment of her, partly at the idea that Statham had cross-questioned her as to why she had permitted the intimacy with Wetter to arise. Wetter himself was annoyed at Statham's presence on the scene, while Humphrey Statham went away sorry and sick at heart at all he had seen and heard. The old stories concerning Wetter which floated about society had reached his ears, and the recollection of them rushed upon him as he sat in the cab on his homeward drive. 'How had this man managed to get a footing in Alice's house; a footing he had evidently obtained, for he spoke of frequent visits there, and his manner was that of an habitué of the house? He was introduced as Madame Du Tertre's cousin; but if that were so, that fact, instead of inspiring confidence in him, was simply sufficient to create distrust of Madame Du Tertre. He was the last man with whom any woman, young and inexperienced, more especially any woman in Alice Claxton's position, should be brought in contact.'

What was best to be done? For an answer to this question Humphrey Statham racked his brain that night. In any case he must write a full account of what he had seen, and of the inference he had drawn therefrom to Martin Gurwood. Martin may not be able to give him any advice, but it was due to him to let him know what had occurred. He, in his simplicity, may see nothing in it; but at all events he must never be able to plead that he was unadvised and unwarned. So before retiring to his rest that night, Humphrey Statham sat down and wrote to his friend a full account of his visit, with a candid statement of the fears and reflections which the presence of such a man as Mr. Wetter in Alice Claxton's household had aroused in him.

'To you,' he said—'to you who have nothing in your life to repair, all this may seem very strained; but I, who have *passé par-là*, and have failed to save one whom I might have saved, know what a sting a failure may come to mean for all the days of a man's life.'

'Nothing in my life to repair!' cried Martin Gurwood, after he had read the letter, clasping his hands above his head.   'My God, if there were but any place for repentance, any possibility of reparation!'

CHAPTER V.

IT was full time that Martin Gurwood returned to Lullington, for his parishioners had begun to grow impatient at his absence. Although, as we have already shown, the Vicar could not be called popular amongst them, having no tastes in common with theirs and rather awe-ing them with his dignified reserve, the good people of Lullington had become accustomed to their parson's ways, and were disposed to overlook what they thought the oddity of his manners in consideration of his bountiful kind-ness and the strict fidelity with which he dis-charged the duties of his office. He was not one of their own sort; he was not a 'good fel-low;' there was nothing at all free-and-easy about him; no jokes were cracked before him;

no harvest-home suppers, no Christmas merry-
'makings found him among the assembled company.   But the farmers, if they did not like
their Vicar, respected him most thoroughly,
and thought it something to have amongst
them a man on whose advice on all spiritual
matters (and in all worldly matters, few indeed though they be, in which honour and
honesty are alone concerned) they could fully
and firmly rely.   So that when Martin Gurwood, on his mother's invitation, went up to
London in the autumn of the year, intending
to stop there but a very few weeks, the church-
wardens and such others of his parishioners as
he deigned to take so far into his confidence,
were sincere in expressing their wishes for his
speedy return.

But if the inhabitants of Lullington were
sorry for their pastor's departure at the time
of his leaving them, much more bitterly did
they regret it after they had had a little experience of his locum tenens.   The gentleman
who had temporarily undertaken the spiritual
care of the Lullingtonians was a man of birth

and ability, an old college friend of Martin Gurwood, and emphatically a scholar and a gentleman. He had married when very young, and had a large family; he was miserably poor, and it was principally with the view of helping him that Martin had requested him to fill his place during his absence. Mr. Dill was only too glad to find some place which he could occupy rent-free, and where he had a better chance of being able to work undisturbed by the racket of his children than in the noisy lodging in town. So he moved all his family by the third-class train, and in less than an hour after their arrival the boys were playing hockey on the lawn, the girls were swinging in the orchard, Mrs. Dill was in her usual state of uncertainty as to where she had packed away any of the 'things,' and Mr. Dill, inked up to the eyebrows and attired in a ragged grey duffel dressing-gown, was seated in Martin Gurwood's arm-chair hard at work at his Greek play.

Although not much given to cultivating politeness, the Lullington farmers, out of re-

spect for Martin Gurwood, thought it advisable
to tender a welcome to their Vicar's representative, and appointed two of their number to
carry out the determination.   The deputation
did not succeed in obtaining admittance; Mr.
Dill's old servant, a kind of female Caleb
Balderstone, meeting them in the hall and
declaring her master to be 'at work'—a condition in which he was never to be interrupted.   The deputation retired in dudgeon,
and that evening at the Dun Cow described
their reception amidst the sympathising groans
of their assembled friends.   It was unani-
mously decided that when Mr. Dill called
upon any of them he should be accommodated
with that species of outspoken candour which
was known in those parts as 'a piece of their
mind.'   It is impossible to say what effect this
intended frankness would have had upon the
temporary occupant of the Lullington pulpit,
inasmuch as that during his whole time of
residence Mr. Dill never called on one of the
parishioners.   Many of them never saw him
except on Sundays; others caught glimpses

of him, a small homely-looking man, striding
about the garden dressed in the before-men-
tioned ragged morning-gown, very short pep-
per-and-salt trousers, white socks not too
clean, and low shoes, gazing now on to the
ground, now into the skies, muttering to himself, and apparently enforcing his arguments
with extended forefinger, but so entranced
and enrapt in his cogitation as to be conscious
of nothing passing around him, or to gaze
placidly into the broad countenances of Hodge
or Giles staring at him over the hedge, without the least notion that they were there. On
Sundays, however, it was a very different
matter. Then Mr. Dill was anything but pre-
occupied. He gave himself up entirely and
earnestly to the duty of addressing his congregation; but he addressed them with such
ferocity, and the doctrine which he preached
was so stern and uncompromising—so different from anything that they had been accustomed to hear from the gentle lips of Martin Gurwood—that the congregation, for the
time struck rigid with awe and dismay, no

sooner found themselves outside the porch than they gathered into a knot in the church-yard and determined on writing off at once to their Vicar to request him to remove his substitute.

The letter, in the form of a round-robin, was duly signed and dispatched, and produced a reply from Martin, counselling moderation, and promising the exertion of his influence with Mr. Dill. That influence had a some-what salutary effect, and on the next Sunday the discourse was incomprehensible instead of denunciatory in its tone. But there was no sympathy between Mr. Dill and those with whom his lot was cast, and spiritual matters in Lullington had come to a very low ebb in-deed when Martin Gurwood returned to his parishioners. Then they revived at once. The Vicar's arrival was hailed with the great-est delight; he was greeted with a cordiality which he had never before experienced, and, after the celebration of service on the ensuing Sunday, there was quite a demonstration of affection towards him on the part of the warm-hearted, if somewhat narrow-minded, people, amongst whom he had not laboured in vain.

But when the gloss of renewed confidence and regard began to wear off, it was noticed among the farmers that the Vicar's reserve, which had been the original stumbling block to his popularity with his parishioners, had, if anything, rather grown than decreased since his visit to London. Martin Gurwood did his duty regular as heretofore; attended schools, visited the sick, was always accessible when wanted; but he seemed more than ever anxious to escape to his solitude; the services of the Irish mare were brought into constant requisition, and she was ridden harder than ever. All this was not lost upon the observant eye of Farmer Barford.

'It's pride, that's what it is, my boy,' said the old man to his son; 'it was so when parson first came down here, and though he got the better of it, it is so again now. It's after having been up to London, and seeing the ways, and wickedness, and goings-on of the grand folks that leaves the sting of envy be-

hind, mebbe; and he knows it's not right, and
flies from the temptation back to these quiet
parts; and then the thought of what he has
seen, and what he has to give up, rankles and
galls him sorely.'

Farmer Barford was by no means strictly
correct in his impression. There was a temptation in London for Martin Gurwood indeed,
but it was not of the kind which the worthy old churchwarden imagined; and though
the Vicar devoted the greater portion of his
thoughts to it, it had not, at first at least,
the effect of goading or harassing him in any
way. Indeed, instead of attempting to expel
the subject from his mind, he loved to brood
and ponder over it, turning it hither and
thither, dwelling upon it in its every phase,
and parting from it to enter once more upon
the work-a-day duties of the world with the
greatest reluctance.

Yes, however much he had attempted to deceive himself when in Alice's presence, to tell
himself that the interest he felt in her merely
arose from pity for the position in which, by

a sad combination of circumstances, she had
been placed, Martin Gurwood no sooner found
himself in the peaceful retreat of his own home,
no longer surrounded by the feverish excitement of London, no longer compelled to be
constantly on his guard lest he should-betray
the Claxton mystery to his mother, lest even
he should betray to his friend Statham the
secret of his heart, than he acknowledged to
himself that he loved Alice. Loved her with
depth and intensity such as no one would have
accredited him with; loved her with a power
of love such as he had never dreamed of possessing, and which astonished him by its force
and earnestness. He, the man of saintly reputation, loved with his whole heart this woman, whose name and fame—innocent, and
even ignorant of it as she was—were tarnished
in the eyes of the world, and quite humbly
put to himself the question if he could win
her. In the silent watches of the night, or
when riding far away from home, he would
bring his horse to a stand-still on wind-swept
common or barren moorland, and ask himself

if he dared—having reference to his own
past life—to hope for such happiness. Surely
there could be little to cause trouble or anxiety to such a man? he, if any one, could afford to stand the scrutiny of the world, could
ignore or laugh at what the world might say
respecting his choice of a wife! And what
could the world say? The secrecy which had
been maintained about the whole matter had
been perfect, so perfect as to make him easy
about the fact that the dead man whom Alice
had believed to be her husband was his step-
father. No one will ever know that but Statham, who is to be trusted, and—and Madame
Du Tertre. He had forgotten her, and somehow, at the thought of her his heart turned
chill within him. She could be relied upon,
however, and Alice would never be troubled
by any one or anything more when once he
had the right to protect her.

To protect her, to watch over and tend
her! To listen to the outpourings of her
mind, simple and innocent as those of any village girl, to mould her soft nature and note

the growth and development under his tui-
tion of the common sense and right feeling
which were her undoubted natural gifts.   To
solace the dead dull level of his daily life with
her sweet companionship; to listen, as he had
never hoped to listen, to words of love addressed to him—to him whose celibate life had
been so long uncheered by fond look or word
of affection!   Could it be possible that this
girl, of whom, as he recollected with something
like dismay, he had at first conceived so dis-
torted an idea, of whom he had spoken with
so much harshness, and to whom he had so
grudgingly extended the common Christian
charity due from him in his position to any
fellow-creature however erring;—could she,
by the mysterious dispensation of Providence,
be the one woman reserved as his haven of
rest from the buffets of the world, as the hope
and comfort of his declining days?   Could
such a blessing come to him?   The whisper of
his fate within him seemed to answer, 'No!'

And yet why should such happiness be
denied him?   However lonely had been his

own life, there were few men who had greater
opportunities of studying the pleasures of do-
mesticity; fewer still more calculated to enjoy
the calm blessings of the married state, all-
sufficient, all-engrossing in themselves.   And
Alice, what response could she make to this
affection? She was surely heart-whole so far
as the present was concerned; she loved no
other man; her affection, such as it was, was
buried in the grave. Such as it was! Yes, the
phrase was harsh-sounding, but true.   Communing with himself, Martin Gurwood came
to the conclusion that Alice during her life
long had never known what it was really to
love.   There could be no doubt, from all he
had heard, from all he had seen, that she had
been devoted to John Calverley, but it was the
devotion of a young girl to a man many years
her senior—to a man with whom their disparity of years prevented her having much in
common.   The feeling which she had entertained for John Calverley was respect, gratitude, affection if you will, but it was not love.
Even if it had been, even if those philosophers,

according to whose dicta the first impression made upon a woman's heart by a man, no matter of what age or position, remains for ever branded and ineffaceable, were right— if Alice had been devoted to John Calverley in a sense other than that which he felt inclined to believe—Martin Gurwood acknowledged that he would be only too glad to take her as she was. He would accept with infinite thankfulness such a love as she could give him, and perhaps it would be better so. The dangerous passion which might have been, he would not ask for, he would not dream of. A quiet trusting love, such as her gentle nature could feel so truly, could give so freely, would amply satisfy him; and notwithstanding the never-ceasing whisper of his fate, he inclined to hope that he eventually might obtain it.

This hope, not arrived at until after many days' anxious self-communing, brought with it a different train of thought—a better train of mind. He was no longer inclined to be solitary now; he took a pleasure in going among his parishioners; in chatting with the old dames and young lasses; in listening to the farmers, and discussing future plans with them. That was to be the scene of his future labours; that was to be the place where his life with Alice would be passed. He pictured her to himself dispensing her charities, aiding him in his work, proving herself, as she was certain to do, kind, patient, active, exactly fitted for a parson's wife. Far removed from London and its temptations, out of the reach of any who might chance to know her previous history, worshipped and protected by him; the benefactress of the poor and sick; the kindly friend of all; her life at Lullington would be as it ought to have been from the first. And his life? It was almost too much happiness to speculate upon it. With the new hope came renewed health, fresh brightness, unaccustomed geniality. His village friends had never before seen their Vicar so radiantly happy; and farmer Barford bade his son Bill remark that all the direful effects of the visit to London had passed away, and that the

Lullington air and the return to his congregation had made their parson a man again.

This happy frame of mind was, however,
not destined to last long. One bright winter's
morning, when Martin Gurwood was walking
briskly up and down the long gravel path
leading to the garden-gate, now and then
diverging for a moment to speak to the old
gardener, who was pottering away in the con-
servatory, and who had as yet scarcely got
over his grief for the damage done to his
favourite shrubs by Mr. Dill's mischievous
children, the heavily-laden village postman
saluted the Vicar, and handed him two letters
and his weekly copy of the *Guardian*. There
was a time when Martin, in his eagerness to
plunge into his journal, would have laid the
letters aside for a more favourable opportunity, but now the postman had become a
person of the greatest interest to him. On
several occasions he had received a letter
from Alice—quietly, simply, and naturally
written—describing the domestic events of
her daily life, and always speaking gratefully

of his kindness towards her.   This morning, however, there was nothing from Alice; one of the letters was written in his mother's narrow-cramped characters; the other in the bold flowing hand of Humphrey Statham.

Martin now never saw his mother's writing without a certain nervous apprehension. However cleverly their precautions had been taken, there was always the chance of Mrs. Calverley's discovering the story of the Claxton mystery, and her son never opened one of her letters without the dread of learning that that discovery had been made.   The perusal of the first lines, however, reassured him on that point, though the letter on the whole was not especially gratifying.

Thus it ran :

'*Great Walpole-street, Wednesday.*

'MY DEAR MARTIN,—Although I have been gifted with a singularly patient disposition, with the power of enduring a large amount of weariness and suffering without complaint, yet

as a worm will turn, so do I at length lift up
my voice to protest against my son's treatment of me. There are not, I imagine, many
mothers in this world who have made such
sacrifices for their offspring as I have for you,
Martin; there are certainly very few sons who
have received such an offer from their parents
as that made by me to you when last you
were in London, and yet the treatment which
I receive at your hands is in exact conformity
with that which has been my lot during my
ill-fated life. My long-suffering has been
overlooked, my kindness unappreciated, my
actions misunderstood.

'Martin, are you, or are you not, going to
take advantage of the offer which I made you
to take your position in my establishment,
give up your country parish, and become a
shining light in the metropolis? One would
have thought such an opportunity, combining
as it would an admirable position in society,
not vain and frivolous, but solid and respectable and eminently fitted for a clergyman,
with the command of wealth, which would

have placed you entirely at your ease, would
have been such a one as you would not have
hesitated to avail yourself of; and yet weeks,
I may say months, have passed since I first
broached the subject to you, and I have as
yet received no definite reply.   I must ask
you to let me hear from you at once, Martin,
upon this point.   I always thought the late
Mr. Calverley the most dilatory of men, and
I do not wish to see his bad example imitated
by my own flesh and blood.

'I suppose that, independently of other
considerations, the son of any other woman
would have thought of his mother's loneli-
ness, and done his best to console her even
under much less agreeable circumstances; but
I am fated I know, and I do not repine.   One
thing, however, I am determined on, and that
is, I will not bear this solitude any longer;
I must have a companion of some kind; and
upon your answer will depend what steps I
shall take.   By the way, talking of companions,
Madame Du Tertre has called here once or
twice lately.   She seems very comfortable in

her new place, and talked a great deal about you. But I have no fear; my son will always know his proper position in society. Write to me at once, Martin; and believe me

'Your affectionate mother,

'JANE CALVERLEY.'

A faint smile played over Martin's lips as he perused two or three portions of this letter, and when he came to its conclusion he laid it aside with a shrug of the shoulder.

'Poor mother,' he muttered, 'she is right so far. I certainly ought to have given her an answer upon that matter long since. I will write to her to - night. Now let's see what Statham has to say.'

The letter from Statham was that described in a previous chapter. Martin's exclamation on reading it has been already recorded. After a little time he placed both letters in his pocket, clasped his hands behind him, and walked up and down the gravel path.

'I must go to London at once,' he said.

' I will answer this letter in person. Statham would not have written in this way if he had not imagined that there were some danger. This man must be paying Alice no ordinary attention if Humphrey's suspicions are excited. I will go to London at once, and take the opportunity of seeing my mother at the same time.'

The next day Martin Gurwood presented himself in 'Change-alley, and was told by Mr. Collins that Mr. Statham was in, and would see him.

CHAPTER VI.

AN EXPLOSION.

In what he called his dreary solitude in South Audley-street (the landlord being of a different opinion, who was accustomed to mention it as elegant quarters for a nobleman or private gentleman, and to charge three hundred a year for the accommodation), Mr. Henrich Wetter was walking to and fro, just as Martin Gurwood, tired out by his night's journey, was beginning to open his eyes and to realise the fact that he was in the Great Northern Hotel. Now sipping his coffee, now nibbling at his dry toast, while all the time achieving his toilet, Mr. Wetter communed with himself. His thoughts were of a pleasant character no doubt, for there was a smile upon his face, and he occasionally suspended his operations both of breakfasting and dressing, in order to rub his hands softly together in the enjoyment of some exquisite sly joke.

'I think so,' he said, pausing in his walk, leaning his elbows on the velvet mantelpiece of the sitting-room, and regarding himself approvingly in the looking-glass; 'I think the time has come for me to bring this little affair to a crisis; dalliance is very delightful for boys; the bashful glances, the sidelong looks, the tremulous hand-clasps, and all that sort of thing, are very charming in one's youthful days, but as one advances in life one finds that procrastination in such affairs is a grand mistake; either it is to be, or it is not to be; and it is advisable to know one's fate, to "put it to the touch, and win or lose it all," as the poet says, as speedily as possible. I rather think it is to be in this instance. The young lady, who chooses to pass herself off as Mrs. Claxton, is remarkably quiet and demure; I should almost be inclined to characterise her as one of those English bread-and-butter misses, if I had not been acquainted with her antecedents. "Yes," and "No, thank you," and "O, indeed!"—that is about the average style of her conversation; no apparent appreciation of anything spiritual; no smart reply; no œillade; nothing piquante or provocative about her; compared to a Frenchwoman or a New-York belle, she is positively insipid; and yet she has fascinated me in a way that is quite inexplicable to myself. It is not her beauty; for, though she is undoubtedly pretty in her simple English style, I have known hundreds of more beautiful women. I think the charm must lie in that very want of manner of which I have just been complaining; in her modesty and quiet grace, and in the complete absence of her knowledge of her own powers of attraction; but whatever it may be, it has had an enormous effect upon me, and I believe myself to be more in love with her than I have been for many years with any woman.

'She likes me too I think, if one can judge by the manner of any one so thoroughly undemonstrative. She always makes me welcome when I call at the house, and accepts, passively indeed, but still accepts, such small courtesies as I have thought it right to offer her. A woman like that, accustomed to affection and attention—for I have no doubt old Calverley was very fond of her in his way—must necessarily want something to cling to, and Alice has nothing; for though she is very fond of little Bell, the child is not her own flesh and blood, and here I have the whole field clear to myself, without any fear of rivalry; for I do not count Humphrey Statham as a rival,' continued Mr. Wetter, as a contemptuous smile passed across his face, 'though he is evidently deeply smitten. I can judge that by the manner in which he scowled at me the other evening when he found me comfortably seated there, and by the awkward uncouth manners, mainly consisting of silent glaring, which an Englishman always adopts whenever he wants to ingratiate himself with a woman. No, no, Mr. Humphrey Statham, yours is not the plan to win little Alice's heart. Besides, if I find you making too much play, I could command the services of

my dear cousin; I could insist that Madame
Du Tertre, my old friend Mademoiselle Pauline Lunelle, should interest herself on my side,
and she has evidently immense influence over
the little woman.

'I think,' said Mr. Wetter, softly stroking
his long fair beard as he surveyed himself in
the glass, 'I think I will go up to Pollington-
terrace about mid-day to-day; I am looking
very well, and feeling bright and in excellent
spirits; and as my plan is well conceived and
well matured, there is no reason why I should
any longer delay putting it into execution.
It would be advisable, however,' said he, re-
flecting, 'that my dear cousin should not be
in the house at the moment of my visit; I will
send down a note to her begging her to come
and see me in the City—a hint which I think
she will not dare to disobey; and while she is
making her way eastward, I will go over to
Pollington-terrace.'

Mr. Wetter came to this determination,
and to the conclusion of his dressing and his
breakfast simultaneously. He then called a

cab, and proceeded to the City, having the satisfaction on his way thither of passing another cab proceeding in the same direction, in the occupant of which he recognised Humphrey Statham. The two gentlemen exchanged salutations; Mr. Wetter's being bland and courteous, Mr. Statham's short and reserved; but Mr. Wetter was very much tickled at the thought of their having met on that particular day, and the smile of satisfaction never left his face until he arrived at his office. Once there, he threw himself into his business with his accustomed energy, for no thought of pleasure passed, or gratification in store, ever caused him to be the least inattentive to the main chance; foreign capitalists and English merchants, flashy promoters of fraudulent companies, and steady-going sober bank directors—men from the West-end, who, filled with the stories of fabulous fortunes made by City speculations, and believing in Henrich Wetter's widespread renown, came to him for advice and assistance; members of parliament and peers of the realm—all of these had inter-

views with Mr. Wetter during the two hours
which he chose that day to devote to business,
and all found him clear-headed, and apparently without thought for any other matter
than that which each submitted to him. But
when the clock on his mantelpiece pointed to
the hour of one, there was scarcely any occasion for him to look to it, for the great rush
of pattering feet down the court which his
window overlooked, and in which a celebrated
chop-house was situate, informed him that the
clerks' dinner-hour had arrived; and Mr. Wetter rang his bell, and, summoning his private
secretary, intimated his intention of striking
work for the day. The confidential young
gentleman, too well trained to say anything at
this unwonted proceeding on his employer's
part, found it impossible to prevent his expressing his surprise by an elevation of his
eyebrows—a movement which Mr. Wetter did
not fail to observe, though he made no com-
ment on it, but he closed his desk, and washed
his hands leisurely, chatting to his companion
meanwhile; and then effecting his retreat by

the private staircase—for it was not advisable that the clerks should see their chief's departure—he stepped into the street, and hailing a cab was driven away to Pollington-terrace.

Mr. Wetter's self-communings while riding in the cab were much of the same kind as those which had occupied him during his morning's toilet. He had directed his driver to take a back route and to avoid the main thoroughfare, lest he should be seen by Pauline on her journey down to the City; and there was comparatively so little traffic along the gaunt streets and in the grim old squares through which he passed, that his attention was not distracted, and the current of his thoughts but little disturbed. He would make his formal declaration that day; he had determined upon that; he should tell Alice that he loved her, that he had in vain struggled against the passion which she had inspired in his breast the first time he accidentally saw her, now some time ago, in the garden at Rose Cottage. She would listen, blush, and

probably be moved to tears; she would talk
about marriage, of course—that was always
the way with women in her position—and he
would fence lightly with the subject, giving
her no positive assurance either way. Not
that the idea of marrying Alice had ever entered into his mind, but that he thought it
would be better to avoid the discussion, certainly to avoid the trouble of having to prove
to her how impossible it would be for him to
take such a step until he had established himself more firmly in her favour. There would
be little difficulty in the matter, he thought,
though more than if she were a woman of
expensive tastes and luxurious habits. That
her manner of life, simple and modest as it
was, seeemed to satisfy her, Mr. Wetter regarded as the most adverse element in the
plan of his campaign; but she would naturally desire to be once more the mistress of a
pretty house, such as she had inhabited when
he first saw her, and to be freed from the
companionship and supervision of Madame
Du Tertre. To suggest that by accepting his

offer she could be released from the enforced
company of that lady was, Mr. Wetter thought,
a great stroke of generalship.

He alighted from the cab at the corner of
the terrace, according to his custom, for his
tact told him that the frequent arrival of
gentlemen visitors in hansom cabs was likely
to scandalise Mrs. Claxton in her neighbours'
eyes, and walked quietly up the street. To
Mr. Wetter such expeditions were by no
means rare, and if any one had told him he
would have been nervous, he would have
laughed in his informant's face; but, to do
him justice, he felt a certain inward trepidation, and, though a cool wintry breeze was
blowing, he raised his hat and wiped the per-
spiration from his brow as he stood upon the
door-step after ringing at the bell. He asked
for Madame Du Tertre at first, and his surprise and slight annoyance at learning that
she was from home were admirably feigned.
Then he asked for Mrs. Claxton. The servant
recognised him as one of the few regular visitors to the house, as the only one, moreover,

who had been in the habit of placing largess
in her sooty palm, and as a nice, well-dressed,
good-looking gentleman at all times. 'Mrs.
Claxton was at home,' she said. 'Would he
walk in?'

Mr. Wetter's nervous trepidation increased
as he heard the street-door close behind him,
and he was glad when he found himself alone
in the room to which he was ushered, the servant retiring and promising to let her mistress
know of his advent. Examining himself in
the glass, he saw that he was paler than usual,
and that his nether lip trembled.

'It's a deuced odd thing,' he muttered, 'I
never felt like this before. I wish there was a
glass of brandy handy. What can there be in
this woman to upset a man like myself, so
perfectly accustomed to such matters?'

The next moment Alice entered the room.
Mr. Wetter had admired her from the first
time he set eyes upon her, but thought he
had never seen her looking so lovely as now,
with her healthy red and white complexion
set off by her black dress; her shining head

with its crisp ripples of dark brown hair, and her hazel eyes, in which a deep, settled, somewhat mournful look had succeeded to the ever-flashing brightly glances of yore. There was something of an air of constraint about her as she bowed to Mr. Wetter and timidly held out her hand.

'You are surprised to see me, Mrs. Claxton, are you not?' said Wetter, doing his best to conquer the nervousness which still beset him—'to see me at such a time of the day, I mean. I have hitherto availed myself of the privilege of calling upon you in the evening, which, on account of my being a busy man, you were good enough to extend to me; but, having occasion to be in this neighbourhood, I took advantage of the opportunity to inquire after your health.'

Alice murmured something to the effect that she was much obliged to him, but Mr. Wetter's quick eye detected that she too was nervous and uncomfortable. And Mr. Wetter thought that this was not a bad chance.

'I am sorry,' said Alice, after a slight pause, 'that Madame Du Tertre is not within.'

'I am also sorry to miss my cousin,' said Mr. Wetter, 'she is always so spirituelle, so amiable. But, to tell the truth, my visit of to-day was not to her, and even had she been at home, I should have asked to see you.'

'To see me, Mr. Wetter! And why?'

'Because, Mrs. Claxton, I have something to say to you, and to you alone. A woman even of your small experience,' he continued, with the faintest sneer playing round his mouth, cannot fail to have observed that you have made upon me more than an ordinary impression; that even during our brief acquaintance you have inspired me with feelings such as we are not often permitted in our lives to experience.'

Alice was silent. As she listened to his first words, as the tone in which he spoke fell upon her ear, the scene then passing seemed to fade away, and there arose before her mind

a vision of the river-walk along the banks of
the Ouse, just abreast of Bishopthorpe, where
in the calm summer evening Arthur Preston
had insulted her with his base proposal. Mr.
Wetter augured well from this silence, and
proceeded more volubly.

'I have known you longer than you imagine,' he said, 'and have admired you from
the first instant I set eyes upon you. I was
so captivated that I determined at all hazards
to make your acquaintance; and when I had
done so, I discovered that you were more
charming than ever, that I was more hope-
lessly enslaved. And then came the fierce
desire to win you, to take you all to myself,
to hold you as my own, my only love.'

She was silent still, her eyes fixed on
vacancy, though her lips trembled. Henrich
Wetter bent forward and laid his hand upon
her fingers as they twitched nervously in her
lap. 'Alice,' he whispered, 'do you hear
me?'

The touch roused her at once. 'Yes,' she
said, quickly withdrawing her hand from his

as though she had been stung, and rising from her chair, 'I do hear what pains and grieves me in the highest degree.'

'Pains and grieves you, Alice—'

'My name is Mrs. Claxton, and I desire you will call me by it. Yes, pains and grieves me, Mr. Wetter,' she continued in a breaking voice, and with a sudden abnegation of her dignity: 'it is cruel in you, it is not like a gentleman to speak to me in this way without the slightest encouragement, and within six months of my husband's death.'

Not like a gentleman! That phrase, quietly spoken as it was, and without any attempt at dramatic emphasis, cut Henrich Wetter to the soul. He was not a gentleman by birth or breeding, by nature, or even by education —and he knew it. His life was one long struggle to deceive on this point those with whom he was brought into contact. He was always suspecting that his position as gentleman was being called in question, and often he would sit with lowering brow and flaming cheek construing the most innocent observations into personal reflections on himself. Not a gentleman! For an instant he winced under the phrase, and then with his blood boiling he determined to be revenged.

He had his voice perfectly under his command as he leant lazily back in his chair and looked up at her.

'Your husband's death!' he echoed. 'Don't you think, Mrs.—Mrs. Claxton, you had better drop all that nonsense with me?'

Alice scarcely understood his words, but there was no mistaking the marked insolence of his tone. 'I—I don't understand you,' she said, in amazement.

'O, yes, you do!' said Mr. Wetter, with the same lazy air. 'I am not Mr. Statham, you know, nor one of your neighbours in the terrace here. I am a man of the world, and understand these matters. Don't talk about dead husbands to me!'

For an instant Alice stood petrified. For an instant a vague idea flashed across her that John might not be dead after all. She had never seen him after death. Could there by any possibility have been a mistake in his identity?

'I don't understand you, Mr. Wetter,' she said, in a low, hurried voice. 'Do you mean to say that my husband, Mr. Claxton, is not dead?'

'I mean to say,' said Wetter, 'what you know very well, that the man with whom you lived in the cottage at Hendon—I saw you there—was not your husband at all.'

Alice bent forward, leaning her hands upon the table, and looking at him for an instant with parted lips and heaving breast. Then she said, 'Not my husband! John Claxton not my husband!'

'John Claxton indeed!' cried Wetter. 'Now, how perfectly ridiculous it is in you to attempt to keep up this nonsense with me! Call the man by his right name—acknowledge him in his proper position!'

She bent nearer to him with her eyes fixed upon his, and said in a low voice, 'Are you mad, or am I?'

In an instant Wetter's intelligence showed

him the real state of the case. This woman was not what he had supposed. She believed herself what she professed to be, the widow of a man named Claxton, not the mistress of dead John Calverley. What should he do? His rage was over, his reason had returned, and he was prepared to act in the way which would best serve his purpose. Should he withdraw from the position he had advanced, getting out of it as best he might, or should he point out to her how matters really stood, the fraud of which she had been the victim, involving her degradation and her shame? That would be the better plan, he thought, for the end he had in view. To destroy her worship of John Calverley's memory, to point out to her how low she had fallen, and then to offer himself as her consoler. That was the best game in his power, and he determined to play it.

His manner had lost all its insolence, all its familiarity, as he courteously motioned her to a seat, and said, 'Sit down, madam, and hear me. Either you are wishing to deceive me,

or, as I rather believe, you have yourself been
made the victim of a gross deception. If the
latter be the case, you will require all your
nerve to bear what I am going to tell you.
The man whom you knew under the name of
Claxton, and whom you believed to be your
husband, was in reality John. Calverley, a
married man, married long since to a woman
of double your age.'

She did not start, she did not cry. She
looked hard at him, and said in a voice that
seemed to force itself with difficulty through
her compressed lips, 'It is not true! It is a lie!'

'It is true—I swear it!' cried Henrich
Wetter. 'I knew Mr. Calverley in business
years ago. Some months before his death I
saw him walking with you in the garden at
Hendon, and recognised him at once. I determined to see you again, but Mr. Calverley's
death intervened, and—' He paused as he
saw Alice pointing towards the door.

'Go,' she said, 'if you please—leave me at
once, I must be left alone.'

Mr. Wetter rose. He had made his coup,

and he knew that then at least there was nothing farther to be done. So he took up his
hat, made a quiet and respectful bow, and left
the room without uttering a word.

Then Alice flung her arms upon the table,
and then burying her head between them, gave
way to the violence of her grief. What wild
exclamations of rage and despair are those
which she utters amidst her bursts and sob-
bings? What reproaches, what maledictions
against him now discovered to be the author
of her misery?

The only distinguishable words are, 'O,
my poor dear John! O, my dear old John!'

CHAPTER VII.

THOU ART THE MAN.

HUMPHREY STATHAM looked up from his writing in astonishment at the sight of his friend.

'Why, Martin,' he cried, rising and extending his hand, 'this is an unexpected pleasure. I thought I might have a line from you some time during the day, but I never anticipated that the letter which I sent you would have the effect of drawing you from your peaceful retreat, more especially as in your last you spoke so strongly in praise of your tranquil existence as contrasted with the excitement and worry here.'

Martin Gurwood recollected that letter. It was written but a few days previously, when his hopes of winning Alice were at their highest, before this element of discord, this stranger of whose presence Statham had warned him, had come into the field. In his friend's re-

mark, however, Martin found something which
instinctively set him on his guard. It would
not do, he thought, to let it be seen how acute
was his interest in the subject on which
Statham had written to him; mere friendship,
mere regard for Alice's welfare would have
contented itself with some far less active demonstration; and though there was no reason
that he knew of for concealing the state of his
feelings from his friend, as he had hitherto
kept them to himself, he thought it was better
not to parade them until some more fitting
opportunity.

So with something like a blush, for the
smallest prevarication was strange to him,
Martin said, ' You must not look upon your
spells as so potent, my dear friend; the same
post which brought me your letter brought
me one from my mother, requesting an immediate decision on a matter which has been
for some time in abeyance, and as this rendered it necessary for me to come to town,
I took advantage of the opportunity to drop
in upon you.'

'I am too pleased to see you to question what has brought you here,' said Humphrey, with a smile, 'and am grateful to Mrs. Calverley for her maternal despotism. And now tell me, what did you think of the news I sent you?'

In spite of the strong effort to the contrary, the flush rose in Martin's cheeks, contrasting ill with the assumed calmness of manner with which he said, 'I received it with great regret.'

'By Jove, Martin, regret is a mild term to express the feeling with which I am inspired in this matter,' said Humphrey Statham vigorously. 'You have seen nothing of what has been going on, nor do I think it likely that with your ignorance of the world and its ways you would have been able to understand it if you had; but I think it desirable that you, whom we have all tacitly placed in the position of Alice's — of Mrs. Claxton's—guardian, should take some immediate action.'

Martin coloured afresh. 'This—this gentleman—' he said.

'Do not misuse a good word,' said Statham,

interrupting him. 'Henrich Wetter, the person of whom we are speaking, is by no means a gentleman in any sense of the term. He is a sharp, shrewd, clever knave, always keeping within the limits of the law, but within those limits thoroughly unscrupulous. He is good-looking, too, and wonderfully plausible; a more undesirable visitor for our friend in Pollington-terrace could scarcely be imagined.'

'And yet he is a cousin of Madame Du Tertre's, and came there through her introduction, I thought you said,' remarked Martin.

'Yes,' said Humphrey, with some hesitation; 'that is a part of the business which I don't quite clearly understand, and on which I have my doubts. There is one thing, however, certain; that is, that he is there very frequently, and that it is advisable he should have a hint to discontinue his visits.'

'And by whom is that hint to be given to him?'

'Of course by Mrs. Claxton. But if her ignorance of the ways of the world prevents her from seeing the necessity of taking such a step, that necessity should be made clear by some one who has the right of advising her. In point of fact—by you !'

'It is my ignorance of the ways of the world upon which you were speaking just now,' said Martin, with a half smile.

'And no one could have a finer theme on which to discourse ; but in certain matters you are good enough to be guided by me.'

'And you say that—'

'I say,' interrupted Humphrey Statham with vehemence, 'that Mr. Henrich Wetter is the last man who should be on intimate visiting terms at Mrs. Claxton's house. He is known not merely to have, but to boast of a certain unenviable reputation which, notwithstanding his undoubted leading position in the business world, causes him to be shunned socially by those who value the fair fame of their womankind.'

'This is bad hearing, indeed,' said Martin Gurwood nervously.

'Bad hearing,' interrupted Statham, emphasising his remark with outstretched hand, 'for any one to whom Alice is—I mean to say for any one who has Mrs. Claxton's interest at heart, it is, indeed, bad hearing.'

Something in the tone of Humphrey Statham's voice, something in the unusual earnest expression of his face, caused Martin to keep his eyes fixed upon his friend with peculiar intensity. What was the reason of the thrill which passed through him as Humphrey had stumbled at the mention of Alice's name? What revelation, which should sting and overwhelm him, was about to be made by the man whose placid and unruffled nature he had often envied, whose heart he had always regarded as a part of his anatomy which did its work well, which beat warmly for his friends, but otherwise gave him little or no trouble?

Humphrey Statham did not keep him very long in suspense. 'Look here, Martin,' said he, 'if you were to tell the people at Lloyd's, that I, Humphrey Statham, of 'Change-alley, was in some respects a fatalist, they would surely laugh at you, and tell you that fatalism and marine insurance did not go very well together. And yet it is to a certain extent the fact. Your arrival here this morning was no chance work, the spirit which prompted you to answer my appeal in person instead of by letter was—there, don't laugh at me—I felt it directly I saw you enter the room, and determined on my course of action, determined on making a clean breast of it, and telling my old friend what I have for some time now been wearing in my heart of hearts.'

He paused, as though expecting his companion to make some remark; but Martin Gurwood sat silent, merely inclining his head, with his hands nervously clutching at the table before him.

'I hardly know how to tell you, after all,' said Humphrey, with something like a blush on such portions of his cheeks as his beard left uncovered; 'and you do not give a fellow the slightest help. You will think it strange in me, queer odd sort of fish that I am, having lived for so many years—for all my life, as far as you know—a solitary, self-contained, oyster-like existence, to acknowledge that I am as vulnerable as other men. But it is so; and on the principle of there being no fool like an old fool, I imagine that my hurt is deeper and more deadly than in ninety-nine other cases. No need to beat about the bush any longer, Martin; I tell you, as my old friend, that I am in love with Alice Claxton.'

Martin Gurwood started. From the time that Humphrey commenced to hesitate, a strange expression had crept over the face of his friend listening to him; but he was so enwrapped in the exposition of his own feelings that he scarcely noticed it.

'You, Humphrey Statham, in love with Alice Claxton!'

'Yes, I! I, whom every one had supposed to be so absorbed in business as to have no time, no care for what my City friends would doubtless look upon as sentimental nonsense. I knew better than that myself; I knew that my heart had by nature been created capable of feeling love; I knew that from experience, Martin; but I thought that the power of loving had died out, never to come again. I was wrong; it has come again, thank God! Never in my life have I been under the influence of a feeling so deep, so true and tender, as that which I have for Alice Claxton.'

As Humphrey ceased speaking, Mr. Collins put his head into the room, and told his chief that Mr. Brevoort was in his carriage at the end of the court, and desired to see him. In an instant Humphrey resumed his business-like manner.

'Excuse me an instant, Martin; Mr. Brevoort is half paralysed, and cannot leave his carriage, so I must go to him. I shall be back in five minutes; wait here and think over what I have just said to you.—Now, Collins!' And he was gone.

Think over what had just been said to him! Martin Gurwood could do that without a second bidding. The words were ringing in his ears; the sense they conveyed seemed clogging and deadening his brain. Humphrey Statham in love with Alice Claxton —with

his Alice — with the woman whom he had
come to look upon as his own, and in whose
sweet companionship he had fondly hoped
to pass the remainder of his life! Her attraction must be great, indeed, if she could
win the affections of such a man as Statham—
calm, shrewd, and practical, not likely to be
influenced merely by a pretty face or an in-
teresting manner. The news came upon Martin like a thunderbolt. In all the long hours
which he had devoted to the consideration of
his love for Alice — to self-probing and ex-
amination—the idea of any rivalry had never
entered into his mind. Not that, owing to
Alice's secluded life or peculiar position, Martin had imagined himself secure; but the idea
had never crossed his mind. She was there,
and he loved her; that was all he knew.
Something like a pang of jealousy, indeed, he
experienced, on reading Humphrey's letter,
telling of Mr. Henrich Wetter's visits to Pollington-terrace; but that, though it had the
effect of inducing him to start for London,
was but a temporary trouble. He had guessed

from what Humphrey wrote, he was sure from what Humphrey said, that this Wetter was not the style of man to captivate a woman of Alice's refinement; and he felt that the principal reason for putting a stop to his visits would be the preventing any chance of Alice's being exposed to annoyance or insult.

But what he had just heard placed matters in a very different light. Here was Humphrey Statham avowing his love for Alice; Humphrey, his own familiar friend, whom he had consulted in his trouble when the story of the Claxton mystery was first revealed to him by Doctor Haughton; Humphrey, who had been the first to see Alice with a view of opening negotiations with her at the time when they so misjudged her real character and position, and who, as Martin well recollected, even then was impressed with her beauty and her modesty, and returned to fight her battles with him. Yes, Humphrey Statham had been her first champion; but that was no reason he should be her last. That gave him no monopoly of right to love and tend her. Was

there any baseness, any treachery, Martin
wondered, in his still cherishing his own feelings towards Alice, after having heard his
friend's confession? Let him think it out
then and there; for that was the crowning
moment of his life.

He sat there for some minutes, his head
bowed, his hands clasped together on his
knees. All that he had gone through since
he first heard in the drawing-room at Great
Walpole-street the true story of John Calverley's death; his first feelings of repulsion
and aversion to the woman whom he believed
to have been the bane of his mother's life;
his colloquies with Statham; his first visit to
Hendon; his meeting with Pauline, and their
plot for keeping Alice in ignorance of the fact
that the funeral had taken place : all this
passed through Martin Gurwood's mind during his reverie. Passed through his mind
also a recollection of the gradual manner in
which he softened to the heart-broken, friend-
less girl, recognising her as the victim instead
of the betrayer, and finding in her qualities

which were rare amongst those of her sex
who stood foremost and fearless in the appro-
bation of the world. Was the day-dream in
which he had of late permitted himself to indulge to vanish in this way? Was he to give
up the one great hope of gladdening his life,
the mere anticipation of which seemed to have
changed the current of his being? No; that
was his determination. Humphrey Statham
was the best, the truest, the dearest fellow in
the world; but this was almost a matter of
life and death, in which no question of sentimental friendship should have weight. He
would tell Humphrey frankly and squarely
what were his own feelings for Alice Claxton,
and they would go in then, in rancourless
rivalry, each to do his best to win her. And
as he arrived at this decision the door opened,
and Humphrey Statham returned.

'Well!' he cried, running up in his bois-
terous way with outstretched hands, 'you
have been lost in reflection, I suppose—chew-
ing the cud of sweet and bitter fancy. Not
bitter though, I hope; there is no bitterness

to you, Martin, in my avowal; nor to any
one else, I fancy, for the matter of that, unless it be that precious article, Mr. Wetter.'

'I have been thinking over what you told
me, Humphrey; and I was going to—'

'No, no, not yet. I haven't told you half
I have to say,' interrupted Statham, pushing
his friend back into his chair, and seating
himself. 'Of course you're astonished, living
the life you do, "celibate as a fly in the heart
of an apple," as Jeremy Taylor has it, at any
one's falling in love, and at me more than any
one else. You think I am not formed for that
sort of thing; that I am hard and cold and
practical, and that I have been so all my life.
You little dream, Martin—for I have never
said a word about it, even to you—that some
years ago I was so devoted to a woman as to
be nearly heartbroken when she abandoned
me.'

'Abandoned you!'

'Yes.' He shuddered, and passed his hand
across his face. 'I don't like to think about
it even now, and should not recur to it if the

circumstances had not a connection with Alice Claxton.'

'With Alice!' exclaimed Martin, and bending forward eagerly.

'Yes. I must tell you the whole story, or you will not understand it; but I will tell it shortly. Some years ago, down in the north, I fell in love with a pretty girl below my own station in life. I pursued the acquaintance, and speedily let her know the state of my feelings towards her; not, as you will readily understand, with any base motives; for I never, thank Heaven, had any desire to play the seducer— What's the matter, Martin? How white you look! Are you faint?'

'A little faint, thank you; it's quite over now. You were saying—'

'I was saying that I despised the wretchedly-vulgar artifices of the seducer, and that I meant fairly and honourably by this girl. I was not able to marry her immediately, however. I was poor then, and her friends insisted, rightly enough, that I should show I was able to maintain her. I worked hard

to that end,' said Humphrey after a short
pause; 'but when I went down in triumph
to claim her, I found she had fled from Headingly.'

'From where?' cried Martin, starting forward.

'Headingly, near Leeds; that was where
she lived. She had fled away from there, no
one knew whither. A week before I reached
the place she was missed—had vanished, leaving no letter of explanation, no trace of the
route she had taken. And I never saw her
more.'

He paused again; but Martin Gurwood
spoke not, bending forward still with his eyes
fixed upon his friend.

'Poor girl—poor darling girl!' muttered
Humphrey, as though communing with himself. 'What an awful fate for one so young
and pretty!'

'What fate?' cried Martin Gurwood.
'Where is she now?'

'Dead,' said Humphrey Statham solemnly.
'Found killed by cold and hunger, with her

baby on her breast. It seems that my poor Emily, deserted by the scoundrel who had se-duced her—may the eternal—'

'Stay!' interrupted Martin Gurwood, wildly throwing up his arms; 'stay! For mercy's sake, do not add your curses to the torture which I have been suffering under for years, and which culminates in this moment!'

'You!' said Humphrey, starting back; 'you! Are you mad?'

'I would to heaven I were! I would to heaven I had been; for I should have had some excuse! The girl you speak of was called Emily Mitchell. I was the man who entrapped her from Headingly; I was the man who ruined her, body and soul!'

Humphrey Statham fell back in his chair; his lips parted, but no sound came from them.

'It is right that you should hear all now,' said Martin in a dull low tone; 'though until this instant I never knew who was the man whom I had wronged so deeply; never, of course, suspected it was you. She told me that there was a gentleman far above her sta-

tion in life who intended to marry her; but
she never mentioned his name. I was on a
visit to a college friend when I first saw Emily
and fell in love with her. I had no evil in-
tentions then; but the thing went on from
bad to worse, until I persuaded her to elope
with me. Ah, my God!' he cried wildly,
'bear witness to the one long-protracted torture which my subsequent life has been—to
the struggles which I have made to shake off
the hypocrisy and deceit under whose do-
minion I have lived, and to stand confessed
as the meanest of Thy creatures! Bear witness to these, and let them plead for me!'

Then he flung himself forward on the
desk, and buried his face in his hands. There
came a knock at the door. Humphrey Statham, all horror-stricken as he was, rushed
forward to prevent any intrusion. But he
was too late; the door opened quickly, and
Pauline entered the room.

CHAPTER VIII.

THE SEALED PACKET.

SEEING Martin Gurwood's attitude of despair, and the horror-stricken expression on Humphrey Statham's face, Pauline started back in amazement.

'Is it possible,' she cried, 'that some one has been beforehand with me, that you already know the news which I come to bring? But no, that could not be.'

She addressed herself to Martin, but, after a brief glance at her, he had resumed his former attitude, and it was Statham who replied.

'You find us talking over a matter which has caused great surprise and pain to both of us, but it is not one,' he added quickly, seeing her start, 'in which, Madame Du Tertre, you could be interested, or of which, indeed, you could have any knowledge. From what you say you would appear to have some communication to make to us—does it concern Mrs. Claxton?'

'It does, indeed,' cried Pauline, with a deep sigh, and more than ever disconcerted at a glimpse of Martin Gurwood's tear-blurred face, which he lifted up as he heard her words; 'it does, indeed.'

Martin did not say a word, but kept his eyes upon her with a hard stony gaze. But Humphrey Statham cried out:

'For God's sake, woman, speak, and do not keep us longer in suspense! Is Alice ill —has anything happened to her?'

'What has happened to her you will be able to guess, when you read this slip of paper which, on my return from a false errand on which I had been lured, I found in an envelope addressed to me.'

She handed him a note as she spoke. Humphrey Statham took it, and read the following words in Alice's handwriting:

'I have found you and your accomplices out! I know my exact position now, and can guess why I was prevented from seeing John after his death!'

'Good heavens, what can this mean?' cried Martin Gurwood, after Statham had read aloud the words of the note.

'Mean!' said Statham. 'There is one portion of it, at all events, which is sufficiently intelligible. "I know my exact position now;" she has learned what we have been so long endeavouring to hide from her! She knows the exact relation in which she stood with Mr. Calverley.'

'Merciful powers, do you think so?' cried Martin.

'What other meaning could that phrase convey?' said Humphrey Statham. 'I myself have no doubt of it, and I think Madame Du Tertre is of my opinion; are you not, madame?'

'I am, indeed,' said Pauline.

'But where can Alice have learned the secret?' said Martin; 'who can have told it to her?'

'I have no doubt on that point either,'

said Pauline; 'it must have been told to her by Mr. Wetter.'

'Wetter!' cried Martin and Humphrey both at the same time.

'Mr. Henrich Wetter,' repeated Pauline. 'It was he who beguiled me into the City upon a false pretence, and on my return home I learned from the servant that he had been at the house during my absence, and had a long interview with her mistress. Then I recognised at once that I had been gotten out of the way for this very purpose.'

'Your suspicions of this man seem to have been just,' said Martin, turning to Humphrey Statham, and speaking slowly, 'though they did not point in that direction.'

'Yes, as I told you before, I knew him to be a bad fellow, and a particularly undesirable acquaintance for Mrs. Claxton,' said Statham. 'But I confess, Madame Du Tertre, that I do not yet see why you should fix upon Mr. Wetter as the guilty person in the present instance, independently, that is to say, of the fact that he was with Mrs. Claxton in the in-

terval between your leaving home and your
return, during which she seems to have ac-
quired this information.   I should not have
thought that Wetter could have known anything about the Calverley and Claxton mystery.'

'He knows everything that he wants to
know,' cried Pauline with energy; 'he is a
fiend, a clever merciless fiend.   If it were his
interest—and it was, as I happen to know—to
make himself acquainted with Alice's history,
he would learn it at whatever cost of money,
patience, and trouble!   It is he that has done
this and no one else, be sure of that.'

'We must allow then, I suppose,' said
Humphrey Statham, referring to the paper
which he still held in his hand, 'that the discovery which Mrs. Claxton claims to have
made is that of her relations with Mr. Calverley, and it seems likely that she gained the
information from Mr. Wetter, who gave it her
for his own purpose.   I take only a subordi-
nate part in the matter, Martin, as your friend,
but it strikes me that it is for you, as Alice's

guardian, to ask Madame Du Tertre, who has evidently a bad opinion—worse than mine almost—of Mr. Wetter, why, having that opinion, she introduced this man to Alice, and suffered him to become intimate at Pollington-terrace.'

'Why did you do this?' cried Martin, turning almost fiercely upon her. 'You say yourself that this is a bad man, and that nothing will stop him when his mind is once made up to the commission no matter of what crime, and yet you bring him to the house and present him to this girl, whom it was so necessary to shield and protect.'

He spoke so wrathfully that Statham looked up in surprise at his friend, and then glancing with pity at the shrinking figure of Pauline, said, in mitigation:

'You must recollect that Mr. Wetter discovered Madame Du Tertre's address by accident, and that he was her cousin!'

'He is not my cousin,' said Pauline, in a low subdued voice, gazing at Martin with tearful eyes, 'I deceived you in that statement, as in many others about Mr. Wetter, and about myself.'

'Not your cousin!' said Martin; 'why, then, did you represent him to be so?'

'Because he insisted on it,' said Pauline, gesticulating freely; 'because he had a certain hold over me which I could not shake off, and which he would have exercised to my detriment if I had not implicitly obeyed him.'

'But how could he have done anything to your detriment so far as we were concerned?' asked Martin.

'Very easily,' replied Pauline. 'It was my earnest desire for—for several reasons to live in the house with Alice as her companion. And Mr. Wetter would have prevented that.'

'How could he have done so?'

'By exercising the influence which he possessed, and which lay in his acquaintance with a portion of my early life. He would have told you what he knew of me, and you would not have suffered me to remain with Alice.'

'You mean to say—' cried Martin, with a certain shrinking.

'O, don't mistake me,' she interrupted; 'I was never wicked, as you seem to imagine; only the manner of my bringing-up, and the associations of my youth were such that, if you had known them, you might not have thought me a desirable companion for your friend.'

'Let me ask you one question, Madame Du Tertre,' said Humphrey Statham. 'Up to this crisis you have undoubtedly discharged your duties with fidelity, and proved yourself to be Alice Claxton's warm and excellent friend. But what first induced you to seek for that post of companion—what made you desire to ally yourself so closely with this young woman?'

'What first influenced me to seek her out?' said Pauline; 'not love for her, you may be assured of that. When first I saw this girl who has played such a part in my life, her head was resting on the shoulder of a man who, in bidding her adieu, bent down to kiss her upturned face, down which the tears were rolling. And that man was my husband.'

'Your husband!' cried Martin.

'My husband. I knew not who the girl was; I had never seen her before; I had never heard of the existence of any one between whom and my husband there could properly exist such familiarity, and I at once jumped to the conclusion that he was her lover, and I hated her accordingly.'

'But you have satisfied yourself that that was not the case,' asked Humphrey Statham hurriedly.

'O, yes,' said Pauline; 'but not until a long time after I first saw them together, not until, so far as one of them was concerned, any feeling of mine was useless. I determined that if ever I saw this woman again I would be revenged upon her! Fortune stood my friend; I did see her; I became acquainted with the mystery of her story, and thus supplied myself with a weapon which could at any time be made fatal to her; I won your confidence,' turning to Martin, 'and made myself necessary to you all, and then, and not till then, did I discover how ill-founded and unjust had been my suspicions; not till then did I learn, by the merest accident, that Alice, instead of having been the mistress of my husband, who was dead by that time, was his sister.'

'Alice your husband's sister?' cried Martin Gurwood in amazement. 'And you were not aware of that fact until animated by false suspicions you had laid yourself out for revenge upon her?'

'Not until I had gained your confidence,' said Pauline, 'or at least taken the first steps towards gaining it. Not until that night at Hendon, when I was left alone with her, and when, while she was under the influence of the narcotic, I looked through her papers— you see I am speaking frankly now, and am desirous of hiding nothing, however much to my own disadvantage it may be — and discovered her relationship to my dead husband.'

'Who was your husband?' said Martin Gurwood in a softened voice.

'It is not likely that you ever heard of him,' replied Pauline. 'His name was Durham. In his last days he had some connection with the house of Calverley and Co., being sent out as an agent to represent them in Ceylon.'

'Durham!' cried Martin Gurwood. 'Surely I have some recollection of that name. Yes; I remember it all now. He was the man who mysteriously disappeared from on board one of the Peninsular and Oriental Company's ships, and who was supposed to have fallen overboard and been drowned on his passage out.'

'The same,' said Pauline; 'he was my husband.'

'Durham!' cried Statham. 'What was his Christian name?'

'Thomas. All his friends knew him as Tom Durham.

'Tom Durham; I knew him well—at one time intimately; but I had no idea that he was married, much less that you were his wife. I recollect now reading the paragraph about his supposed drowning·the last time I left London on my holiday.'

'You knew Tom Durham well?' cried Pauline, clasping her hands. '*Mon Dieu*, I see it all! You are the H. S., whose letter I have here!'

As she spoke she took a pocket-book from the bosom of her dress, and from it extracted ·a paper, which she handed to Statham.

'That is my handwriting, surely,' said Humphrey, running his eyes over the document. 'In it I acknowledge the receipt of a packet which I promised to take care of, and declare I will not give it up save to Tom himself, or to some person duly accredited by him. The packet is in that iron safe, where it has remained ever since.'

'What do you imagine it contains?' asked Martin.

'I have not the remotest idea,' replied his friend. 'As you will see, by a perusal of this paper, Tom Durham offered to inform me, but

I declined to receive his confidence, partly because I thought my ignorance might be of service to him, partly to prevent myself being compromised.'

'Do you think it could have any bearing upon Alice?' asked Pauline.

'If I thought so, I should not hesitate for an instant to place it in your hands. Whatever may have been the motive by which you were actuated at first, you have been a sure and steady friend to that poor girl, and I have perfect reliance on you.'

'This poor man, Durham, will now never come to claim the packet himself,' said Martin Gurwood, 'and his widow is plainly his nearest representative. If there be anything in it which concerns Mrs. Claxton, we should never forgive ourselves for not having taken advantage of the information which it may contain.'

'You think, then, perhaps on the whole I should be justified in handing it to Madame Du— I mean to this lady,' said Statham.

'Certainly, I think so.'

'So be it,' said Statham, walking round to the desk at which Martin was seated, and taking from the top drawer a key, with which he proceeded to unlock the iron safe; 'there it is,' he added, ' duly marked "Akhbar K," and exactly in the same condition as when I received it from poor Tom's messenger.'

And with these words he placed a packet in Pauline's hands.

She broke the seals, and the outside cover fell to the ground. Its contents were two sheets of paper, one closely written.

'There is nothing but this,' she said, looking though it; then turning to Mr. Statham, 'it will be as well, perhaps,' she said, 'if you were to read it aloud.'

Humphrey took the paper from her hand and read as follows:

'My dear Humphrey Statham,—Within a week after this reaches you I shall have left England for what may possibly prove a very long absence; and although I am pretty well accustomed to a roving life, and have been so busy, that I have never had time to be superstitious, I, for the first time, feel a desire to leave my affairs as much in order as possible, and to put as good a polish on my name as that name will bear.

'After all, however, I do not see that I need inflict a true and particular history of my life and adventures upon a man so busied as yourself. It would not be very edifying reading, my dear Statham, nor do I imagine that being mixed up in any way with my affairs would be likely to do you much good with the governor of the Bank of England or the directors of Lloyd's. I scarcely know how you, a steady, prosperous man of business, ever managed to continue your friendship with a harum-scarum fellow like myself! It was all very well in the early days when we were lads together, and you were madly in love with that Leeds milliner-girl'—Humphrey Statham's voice changed as he read the passage—'but now you are settled and respectable, and I am as great a ne'er-do-weel as ever.

'Not quite so great, perhaps, you will think, when you see that I am going to try to make amends for one wrong which I have done. I shall not bother you with anything else, my dear Statham; but I will leave this one matter in your hands, and I am sure that if any question about it ever arises, you will look to it and see it put straight for the sake of our old friendship, and don't break down or give it up because I seem to come out rather rough at the first, dear old man. Read it through, and stand by me.

'You do not know — nor any one else scarcely, for the matter of that—that I have a half-sister, the sweetest, prettiest, dearest, and most innocent little creature that ever shed sunshine on a household. She didn't shed it long on ours though; for as soon as she was old enough, she was sent away to earn her own living, which she did by be-coming governess in a Quaker's family at York. I was fond of her—very fond in my odd way—but I never saw much of her, as I was always rambling about; and when, after

a return from an absence of many months, I
heard that Alice was married to an elderly
man named Claxton, who was well off, and
lived in comfort near London, I thought it
was a good job for her, and troubled myself
but little more about the matter.

'But one day, no matter how, my suspicions were aroused. I made inquiries, and—
to cut the matter short—I discovered that
the respectable Mr. Claxton, to whom I had
heard Alice was married, was a City merchant, whose real name was Calverley, and
who had already a wife. I never doubted
Alice for a moment; I knew the girl too well
for that. I felt certain this old scoundrel had
deceived her, and, as they say in the States,
"I went for him."

'There's no use denying it, Humphrey, I
acted like a mean hound; but what was I to
do? I was always so infernally hard up. I
brought the old boy to his bearings, and made
him confess that he had acted a ruffian's part.
And then I ought to have killed him, I suppose. But I didn't. He pointed out to me

that Alice was in perfect ignorance of her
real position, that to be informed of it would
probably be her death. And then—he is a
tremendously knowing old bird — he made
certain suggestions about improving my fin-
ancial position and getting me regular employment, and giving me a certain sum of
money down, so that somehow I listened to
him more quietly than I was at first disposed
to do. Not that I wasn't excessively indig-
nant on Alice's account. Don't make any
mistake about that. I told old Calverley that
he had done her a wrong which must be set
right, so far as lay in his power; and I made
him write out a paper at my dictation and
sign it in full, with his head-clerk as witness
to the signature. Of course the clerk did not
know the contents of the document, but he
saw his master sign it, and put his own name
as witness. This was done two days ago, just
at the time when they had been writing a lot
of letters in the office about my taking up
their agency in Ceylon, and no doubt he
thought it had something to do with that.

I shall enclose that paper in this letter, and
you can use it in case of need. Not that I
think old Calverley will go away from his
word; in the first place, because, notwithstanding this rascally trick he has played
poor Alice, he seems a decent kind of fellow;
and in the next, because he would be afraid
to, so long as I am to the fore. But something might happen to him or to me, and
then the paper would be useful.

'Here is the whole story, Humphrey, con-
fided to your common sense and judgment, to
act with as you think best, by

                    'Your old friend,
                              'TOM DURHAM.'

'Something has happened to both of them,'
said Humphrey Statham, solemnly, picking up
the paper which had fluttered to the ground.
'Now let us look at the enclosure:

'I, John Calverley, merchant, of Mincing-
lane and Great Walpole - street, do hereby
freely confess that having made the acquaint-

ance of Alice Durham, to whom I represented myself as a bachelor of the name of Claxton, I married the said Alice Durham at the church of Saint Nicholas, at Ousegate, in the city of York, I being, at the same time, a married man, and having a wife then, and now, living. And I solemnly swear, and hereby set forth, that the said Alice Durham, now known as Alice Claxton, was deceived by me, had no knowledge of my former marriage, or of my name being other than that which I gave her, but fully and firmly believes herself to be my true and lawful wife.

'This I swear,

'JOHN CALVERLEY.

'Witness,

'THOMAS JEFFREYS,

'Head Clerk to Messrs. Calverley and Co.'

'That appears to me decisive as an assertion of Alice's innocence,' said Martin Gurwood, looking round as Humphrey finished reading.

'To most persons it would be so,' said

Statham; 'but Mrs. Calverley, with whom we chiefly have to deal, is not of the ordinary stamp. It will be advisable, however, I think, that we should see her at once, taking this document with us. If Madame Du—if Mrs. Durham's suspicions of Mr. Wetter are well founded, he will not have uttered his bark without being prepared to bite, and it is probably to Mrs. Calverley that he will first address himself.'

'Do you wish me to accompany you?' asked Pauline.

'No,' said Statham, 'I think you had better return home.'

'I think so, too,' said Martin; 'your sister may be expecting you.'

Her sister! In her broken condition it was some small comfort to Pauline to hear the acknowledgement of that connection from Martin's lips.

CHAPTER IX.

In the house in Great Walpole-street there was little change. Things went on in pretty much the same manner as when John Calverley was in the habit of creeping back to his dismal home with sorrow in his heart, or when Pauline sat watching and plotting in the solitude of her chamber. Since her second husband's death Mrs. Calverley seemed to have eschewed even the small amount of society which she had previously kept; the heavy dinner-parties were given up, and the only signs of so-called social intercourse were the fortnightly meetings of a Dorcas Club which was held under Mrs. Calverley's auspices, and at which several elderly ladies of the neighbourhood discussed tea and scandal under the pretence of administering to the necessities of

the poor.   At other times, the mistress of the
house led a life which was eminently solitary
and self-contained.   She read occasionally, it
is true ; but when she called at the circulating
library, she brought away with her, for her
amusement or edification, no story in which,
under the guise of fiction, the writer had en-
deavoured to portray any of the varieties of
shifting human nature which had come beneath his ken ; no poem glowing with passion
and ardour, or sweetly musical with melodi-
ous numbers.   Hard, strong books of travel
through districts with immense upronounce-
able names; tales of missionary enterprise set
forth in the coldest, baldest, and least-educated
style, relieved with frequent interpolations of
theological phraseology ; reviews which had
once been potential, but whose feeble echoes
of former trumpet fanfarons now fell idly on
inattentive ears; polemical discussions on re-
ligious questions, and priestly biographies—
lives of small men, containing no proper precept, setting no worthy example—these were
Mrs. Calverley's favourite reading.   The butler

declared that she read nothing at all; that though these books were brought from Mudie's on the back seat of the carriage, and were afterwards displayed on the drawing-room table, one at a time occupying the post of honour on his mistress's lap, she never so much as glanced at them, but sat staring with her steely blue eyes straight in front of her; a state of things which, rigorously persisted in, afflicted the butler, on his own statement, with a disease known to him as 'the creeps,' and which was considered generally so un-canny throughout the lower regions, that had not the wages been good and the table liberal, the whole household would have departed in a body.

About four o'clock on a dull afternoon in the very early spring, Mrs. Calverley was seated in her drawing-room in that semi-coma-tose state which inspired her domestics with so much terror. Some excuse, however, was to be made for her not attempting, on the pre-sent occasion, to read the book which lay idly in her lap, the time being 'between the lights,'

as the phrase goes, when the gathering gloom
of light, aided by the ever-present thickness
of the London atmosphere, blots out the sun's
departing rays before the time recorded in the
almanac.   It was very seldom, indeed, that
Mrs. Calverley suffered her thoughts to dwell
upon any incident of her immediately passed
life.   On what had happened during her girl-
hood, when she was the spoiled and petted
heiress, on certain episodes in the career of
jolly George Gurwood, her first husband, in
which she had borne a conspicuous part, she
was in the habit of bestowing occasional re-
membrances; but all that concerned her later
life she wilfully and deliberately shut out from
her mind.   And this not from any sting of
conscience, for Mrs. Calverley considered herself far too immaculate to be open to any such
vulgar, consideration, but, as she said to herself, because everything of that kind was too
near to allow her to form an impartial judgment upon it.   It chanced, however, that upon
this particular day, the deceased John Calverley had been frequently present to his widow's

recollection. There was nothing extraordinary in this; it arose from the fact that that
very morning, in looking through the contents
of an old trunk which had long since been
consigned to the lumber-room, Mrs. Calverley
had come upon an old fly-blown water-colour
drawing of a youth with a falling linen collar,
a round jacket, and white-duck trousers, a
drawing which bore some faint general re-
semblance to John even as she remembered
him. Pondering over this work of art in a
dreamy fashion, Mrs. Calverley found herself
wondering whether her late husband's mental
condition in youth had been as frank and in-
genuous as that to be gathered from his physical portrait; and, secondly, whether she had
not either faultily misapprehended or wilfully
misconstrued that mental and moral condition
even during the time that she had been acquainted with him. Two or three times later
in the day her mind had wandered to the
same topic, and now, as she sat in the dull
drawing-room in the failing light, her thoughts
were full on him. It was pleasant, she re-

membered, though she had not thought so at
the time, to be looking forward in expectation
of his return home at a certain hour; pleasant
to know that he would probably be detained
beyond the appointed time, thereby giving her
opportunity for complaint; pleasant to have
some one to vent her annoyance upon who
would feel it so keenly, and reply to it so little.
She had not hitherto looked at her loss from
this point of view, and she was much struck
by the novelty of it; though she had never
had any opinion of Mr. Calverley, she was
willing to admit that he was not absolutely
bad-hearted; nay, there were times when—

Her reverie was interrupted by the en-
trance of the butler, who announced that a
young lady was below desiring to speak to
Mrs. Calverley.

'A lady! What kind of a lady?'

'A—a widow, mum,' replied the butler,
pointing in an imbecile way, first at Mrs. Calverley's cap, and then at his own head.

'Ah,' said Mrs. Calverley, with a deep
groan, and shaking her head to and fro—for

she never missed an opportunity of making capital out of her condition before the servants—'one who has known grief, eh, James? And she wants to see me?'

'Asked first if you lived here, mum, and then was very particular in wishing to see you. A pleasant-spoken young woman, mum, and not like any begging-letter impostor, or coves—or people I mean—of that sort.'

'You can light the gas, James, and then show the lady up. No, stay; show her up at once, and do not light the gas until I ring.'

Since she had known Madame Du Tertre, Mrs. Calverley had taken some interest in her own personal appearance, and not having seen her toilet-glass since the morning, she had an idea that she might have become somewhat dishevelled.

The butler left the room, and presently returned, ushering in a lady who, so far as Mrs. Calverley could make out in the uncertain light, was young, of middle height, and dressed in deep mourning.

The mistress of the mansion motioned her

visitor to a seat, and making a stiff bow
said :

'You wish to speak to me, I believe?'

'I wish to speak with Mrs. Calverley.'

'I am Mrs. Calverley. What is your business?'

'Your—your husband died recently?'

'About six months ago. How very curious! What is your object in asking these
questions?'

'Bear with me, pray! Do not think me
odd; only answer me what I ask you—my
reasons for wishing you to do so are so
urgent.'

The lady's voice was agitated, her manner
eager and unusual. Mrs. Calverley did not
quite know what to make of her visitor. She
might be a maniac, but then why her interest
in the deceased Mr. Calverley? Another, and
to her idea, a much more likely explanation
of that mystery arose in Mrs. Calverley's mind.
Who was this hussy who was so inquisitive
about other women's husbands? She should
like to see what the bold-faced thing looked

like. And she promptly rang the bell to summon James to light the gas.

'You will answer me—will you not?' said the pleading voice.

'It depends upon what you ask,' replied Mrs. Calverley with a smile.

'Tell me then—Mr. Calverley—your husband—was he very fond of you?'

The few scattered bristles which did duty as Mrs. Calverley's eyebrows rose half an inch nearer her forehead with astonishment.

'Yes,' she replied after a moment's reflection; 'of course he was—devoted.'

Something like a groan escaped from the stranger.

'And you—you loved him?'

'Very much in the same way,' said Mrs. Calverley, feeling herself for the first time in her life imbued with a certain amount of grim humour—'quite devoted to him.'

'Yes,' said the visitor sadly, 'that I can fully understand. Did you ever see or hear of his partner, Mr. Claxton?'

'I never saw him,' said Mrs. Calverley;

'I've heard of him often enough, oftener than I like. It was he that persuaded Mr. Calverley to going into that speculation about those iron-works which Mr. Jeffreys can make nothing of. But he wasn't a partner in the house; there are no partners in the house— only some one that Mr. Calverley knew in the City, and probably a designing swindler, for Mr. Calverley was a weak man, and this Claxton—'

'Mr. Claxton was the best man that ever walked this earth!' cried Alice, breaking forth, 'the kindest, the dearest, and the best.'

'Heyday!' cried Mrs. Calverley with a snort of defiance. 'And who may you be, who knows so much about Mr. Claxton, and who wants to know so much about Mr. Calverley?'

'That is right, James,' she added, 'light the gas;' and then she said in a lower tone, 'I shall be better able to judge the kind of visitor I have.'

The gas was lighted and the servant left the room; Mrs. Calverley rose stiffly from her

chair and advanced towards Alice, who remained seated.

'What is this,' she said in a strong voice,
'and who are you ? coming here tricked out
in these weeds to make inquiries, and to utter
sentiments at which modest women would
blush. Who are you, I say ?'

But while Mrs. Calverley had been speaking Alice had looked up, and her eyes had
fallen upon a picture hanging against the wall.
A big crayon head of John, her own old John,
just as she had known him, with the large
bright eyes, the heavy thoughtful brow, and
the lines round the mouth somewhat deeply
graven. For an instant she bent her head before the picture, the next, with the tears well-
ing up into her eyes, and in a low soft voice,
without the slightest exaggeration in tone or
manner, she said :

'You ask me who I am, and I will tell
you!' Then pointing up to the portrait, 'I am
that man's widow!'

'What!' screamed Mrs. Calverley. 'Do
you know who that was ?'

'No,' said Alice, 'except that he was my husband.'

'Why, woman!' exclaimed the outraged mistress of the house, in a torrent of rage, 'that was Mr. Calverley!'

'I know nothing,' said Alice, 'save that in the sight of Heaven he was my husband. Call him by what name you will, he had neither lot nor part with you. You tell me that he loved you, was devoted to you—it is a lie! You talk of your love for him, and that may be indeed, for he was meant to be loved! But he was mine, all mine—ah, my dear John! ah, my darling old John!'

She broke down utterly here, and fell on her knees before the picture, in a flood of tears.

'Well, upon my word,' cried Mrs. Calverley, 'this is a little too much! No one who knows me would imagine for a minute that I should condescend to quarrel about Mr. Calverley with any trolloping miss who chooses to come here! And no one who knew Mr. Calverley, selfish and neglectful as he was, and without the least consideration for me, would suspect him of being such a Bluebeard or a Mormon as you endeavour to make him out! How dare you come here with a tale like this! How dare you present yourself before me with your brazen face and your well-prepared story, unless it is, as I suppose, to induce me to give you hush-money to stop your mouth. Do you imagine for an instant that I am to be taken in by such a ridiculous plot? Do you imagine for an instant that—'

She stopped, for there was a sound of voices outside, and the next moment the door opened and Martin Gurwood, closely followed by Humphrey Statham, entered the room.

Mrs. Calverley dropped the arm which she had extended in monition, and Alice ran to place herself by Martin Gurwood's side.

'Save me from her!' she cried, shrinking on his arm. 'Save me from this woman!'

'Do not be afraid, Alice,' said Martin, endeavouring to calm her. 'We thought to find you here, but hoped to be in time to prevent your suffering any annoyance. Mother,' he added, turning to Mrs. Calverley, 'there is some mistake here.'

'There must be some mistake, indeed,' observed Mrs. Calverley, with great asperity, 'when I find my son, a clergyman of the Church of England, taking part against his mother with a woman who, take the most charitable view of it, is only fitted for Colney Hatch Lunatic Asylum.'

'Not to take part against you, mother? Surely—'

'Well, I don't know what you call it,' cried Mrs. Calverley, 'or whether you consider it quite decorous to keep your arm round that young person before your mother's face! Or whether'—here the worthy lady gave a short nod towards Statham—'gentlemen with whom I have but slight personal acquaintance think themselves justified in coming into my house uninvited! I am an old-fashioned person, and I daresay don't understand these matters, but in my time they would not have been tolerated.'

'See, dear mother,' said Martin quietly,

'you do us all, and more especially this lady, great injustice!'

'O, very likely,' said Mrs. Calverley, sarcastically; 'very likely she is right and I am wrong! She has just told me that she was Mr. Calverley's wife, and no doubt you will bear out that that is correct, and that I have been dreaming for the last twelve years.'

'If you will permit me to speak, madam,' said Humphrey Statham in his deep tones, 'I think I can prove to you that this lady has, or imagines she has, grounds for the statement which she has made, and that while you have been deeply injured, her injuries are worse, and more serious than yours.'

'You will hear Mr. Statham, if you please, mother,' said Martin Gurwood; 'I am here to attest the truth of all that he will say.'

And then, with homely natural eloquence springing from the depth of his feeling, Humphrey Statham told, in nervous unadorned language, the story of the betrayal of the woman whom he loved. On the dead man's perfidy he dwelt as lightly as he could, more

lightly still on the probable causes which had
induced the dead man to waver in his faith,
and to desert the home which had been rendered so unattractive to him; but he spoke
earnestly and manfully of the irremediable
wrong done to Alice, and of the manner in
which her life had been sacrificed; and,
finally, he produced the document in John
Calverley's handwriting, which had just been
discovered, to show how completely she had
been made the victim of a fraud.

Sitting bolt upright on her chair, and
slowly rubbing her withered hands one over
the other, Mrs. Calverley listened to Statham's
speech. When he stopped she bridled up and
said with asperity,

'A very pretty story indeed; very well
concocted and arranged between you all. Of
course, I may believe as much of it as I
choose! There's no law, I imagine, to compel
me to swallow it whole, even though my son,
a clergyman of the Church of England, sits
by and nods his head in confirmation of his
friend. And don't imagine, please, that I am

at all surprised at what I hear about Mr.
Calverley! I hear it now for the first time,
but I always imagined him to be a bad and
wicked man, given up to selfishness and de-
bauchery, and quite without the power of
appreciating the blessings of a well-ordered
home. The young woman needn't start! I
am not going to demean myself by engaging
in any controversy with her, and wish rather
to ignore her presence. But I will say,' said
Mrs. Calverley, drawing herself up, ' but I
will say that I had not expected to find that
my son was sanctioning these proceedings,
and conniving at the disgrace which was
being heaped upon me.'

'Mother!' cried Martin Gurwood, appeal-
ingly.

'It might,' continued Mrs. Calverley, with
great placidity, 'it might have been imagined
that, as my son, and leaving out all question
of his clerical position, he would have adopted
another course, but such do not appear to
have been his views. Let me tell him,' she
cried, turning upon Martin with sudden fierce-

ness, 'that henceforward he is no son of mine;
That I renounce him and leave him to shift
for himself; he has no longer any expectations
from me! On certain conditions I promised
to share all with him now, and leave him my
sole heir at my death. But I revoke what I
said; I am mistress of my own fortune, and
will continue to be so. Not one penny of it
shall go to him.'

'You are, of course, at liberty to do what
you like with your fortune, mother,' said
Martin quietly, 'and it would never occur to
me for an instant—'

'Stay!' interupted Statham, taking his
friend by the arm and pointing to Alice;
'there is no use in prolonging this painful
discussion, and Mrs. Claxton is completely
exhausted.'

'You are right,' said Martin, rising from
his seat, 'we have been somewhat thoughtless
in thus overtaxing her strength, and will take
her home at once.' Then advancing, he said,
in a low tone, 'Mother, will you see me to-
morrow?'

'Mr. Martin Gurwood,' said Mrs. Calverley, in a clear cold voice, ' with my own free will I will never look upon you again! And though the name that I bear is that of one who was a scoundrel, I am glad that it is not the name which is disgraced by you!'

And thus those two parted.

CHAPTER X.

WHEN they reached the street, Humphrey Statham stopped short, and turning to Martin, said, 'You had better see Mrs. Claxton to her home. The excitement of the day has been too much for her, and the sooner she is under the fostering care of Madame Du Tertre—it seems impossible for me to call her by any other name—the less chance there will be of her suffering any ill-effects.'

'Will you not go with us?' asked Martin, looking directly at his friend for the first time since the dread explanation concerning Emily Mitchell had passed between them, and still speaking with nervous trepidation; 'will you not go with us?'

'No,' replied Humphrey, 'not now; there

is something which I think ought to be done, and I am the proper person to do it.'

His manner was so odd that both Alice and Martin were struck by it at once, and the latter, taking Humphrey by the arm, drew him aside for a moment and said,

'I have an idea of what now fills your mind, and of the errand on which you are going. You will not suffer yourself to run into any danger?'

'Danger!'

'I repeat the word—danger! Life has a new happiness in store for you now, Humphrey Statham, and should consequently be more precious than you have ever yet considered it.'

His voice had regained its usual clear tone, and as he spoke he looked frankly in his friend's eyes. In the gaze which met his own, Martin saw that the deadly wrong which he had unwittingly wrought upon his companion was forgiven, and had he doubted it, the grasp with which his hand was seized would have been sufficient proof.

'Don't fear for me, old friend,' said Humphrey, his face glowing with delight at the idea which Martin's words had aroused; 'depend upon it I will run no risks, and neither by word or act give a chance by which I or others could be compromised. But it is necessary that a word of warning should be spoken in a certain quarter, with energy and promptitude. So for the present farewell.'

He turned to Alice as he finished speaking, and raising his hat was about to move away. But she put out her hand to him, and said, with pretty becoming hesitation, 'I cannot thank you as I ought, Mr. Statham, for the manner in which you have just pleaded my cause with—with that lady, any more than I can show my gratitude for the constant kindness I have met with at your hands.'

Humphrey Statham attempted to make a reply, but gave utterance to nothing. The words failed him, and for the first time in his life perhaps he was fairly nonplused. As the sweet young voice rang on his ear, as he felt the pressure of the warm soft hand, a strange

vibration ran through him, and he knew himself on the point of giving way to an exhibition of feeling, the possibility of which a few
months previously he would have laughed to
scorn.   So with a bow and a smile he turned
on his heel and hurried rapidly away.

Martin watched his friend's departing figure for a moment, then with a half-sigh he
said to his companion, 'I am glad that you
spoke your thanks to Humphrey so warmly,
Alice; for he has been your truest and best
friend.'

'Rather say one of them,' said Alice, laying
her hand lightly on his arm; 'you take no
credit to yourself, Mr. Gurwood.'

The colour had faded from his cheeks and
from his compressed lips ere he replied coldly,
'I take as much as is my due.   Now let me
call a cab and take you home, for on our way
there I have something more to say to you.'

'Something more,' she cried, with a frightened air.   'O, Mr. Gurwood, nothing more
dreadful, I hope; nothing that—'

'Do you imagine for an instant that I

would put you to unnecessary suffering,' he
said, almost tenderly, looking down into her
pleading upturned eyes; 'that I, or any of us,
would not shield you from any possible annoyance. No, what I have to say to you will, I
think, be rather pleasant to you than otherwise. Here is the cab; I will tell you as we
go along.'

When they were seated in the vehicle,
Martin said to his companion, 'You have now,
Alice, had Madame Du Tertre for your friend
quite long enough to judge of her disposition,
and to know whether the desire to serve your
interests which she originally professed was
dictated by a spirit of regard for you, or
merely assumed to serve her own purposes.'

'There can be no question in the matter,'
said Alice, almost indignantly; 'nothing can
exceed the devotion which Pauline has exhibited to me ever since we came together. She
is infinitely more like an elder sister to me
than a person whose acquaintance I seem to
have made by the merest chance.'

'There is often more than chance in these

matters,' said Martin gravely; 'more than there seems to be in the chance use of a word. . You have said that Pauline has seemed to you as an elder sister — suppose she really stood to you in that position?

'That could scarcely be,' said Alice; 'for years and years I had no relation but my poor brother, and since his death—'

'Since his death Providence has sent some one to fill his place much more efficiently than he ever filled it himself, so far as you are concerned, my poor child,' said Martin.

And then he told her what had occurred between them and Pauline at Statham's office, omitting, of course, all reference to the jealous feelings by which the Frenchwoman had at first been actuated, and dwelling upon the self-sacrifice and devotion with which she had espoused her kinswoman's cause.

Alice was much touched at this narrative, and when they reached home she embraced Pauline with such tenderness, that the latter knew at once that her story had been told; knew too, that Martin had been silent about the incidents of her early life and the reasons which had originally prompted her to throw herself in Alice's way, and was proportionately grateful to him.

Late that night, when they were together, Alice lying in her bed and Pauline sitting by her side, the two women had a long, earnest, and affectionate talk, in the course of which the strange events which the day had brought to light came under discussion. It was evident to Pauline that Alice had braced herself up to talk of her own position, and of the deception of which she had been the victim; but the Frenchwoman saw that her companion was in no condition to bear the excitement which such a topic would necessarily evoke, and gradually, but skilfully, drew her away from it. The case, however, was different when Alice depicted the rage and consternation of Mrs. Calverley at learning the part taken by her son in the concealment of the Claxton mystery. This was a point in which Pauline took the keenest interest, and she induced Alice to dilate on it at her will, framing

her questions with much subtlety, and pondering over each answer she received. When
Alice stated Mrs. Calverley's intention of dis-
inheriting her son, and leaving him to struggle on in the comparatively obscure position
which he then occupied, something like a ray
of light shot into Pauline's darkened soul.
Should the intention thus announced be carried out, should Martin be left to his own re-
sources, she might then have the chance, such
as never could occur to her under other circumstances, of proving her disinterested love
for him. For the man of wealth, for the man
even with great expectations, she could do
nothing; any advances which she might make,
any assistance which she might offer, the
world would but regard as so much small
bait thrown out for the purpose of securing
a greater booty; and he, knowing as he did
the circumstances of her previous life, the
scheming predatory manner of her early existence, would too surely be of the opinion of
the world. But if he were poor, and broken,
and humbled, grieving over the alienation of

his mother, and feeling himself solitary and shunned, her self-appointed task in winning him, in proving to him her devotion, in placing at his disposal the small means which she had, the worldly talent which even he acknowledged she possessed, would be a very much easier one.

'Mistress of her own fortune, and would continue to remain so; that is what she said, is it?' Pauline asked, after a pause.

'That is what she said, and that she renounced her son, and revoked all the declarations she had hitherto made in his favour,' said Alice. 'Was it not dreadful for poor Mr. Gurwood? I do pity him so.'

'Do you?' said Pauline, turning her searching gaze full upon the girl's face. 'Yes, I daresay you do. It is natural you should; Mr. Gurwood has been a good friend to you.'

'The best—almost the best—I had in the world.'

'Almost the best! Why, who could rank equal with him?'

'Mr. Gurwood himself said Mr. Statham,' cried Alice with downcast eyes.

'Ay, ay,' said Pauline quickly. Then, after an interval of a few minutes, the old cynical spirit coming over her, she added, more as if talking to herself than to her companion, 'I don't think we need trouble ourselves much, for Mr. Gurwood's sake, about that old woman's threat. I know her well; she is hard and cold and proud; but with all those charming qualities, and like many of your rigid English Pharisees, she is superstitious to a degree. She dare not make a will for fear of dying immediately she had signed her name to it; and if she dies without a will, her son inherits all her property. *Vogue la galère!* Mr. Gurwood's chances are not so bad after all. There,' she added, in a softened voice, seeing Alice gazing at her in astonishment, 'get to sleep now, child; you have had a long and trying day, and must be quite wearied out.'

Alice fell asleep almost immediately, but for more than an hour afterwards Pauline sat with her feet on the fender gazing into the slowly dying embers and pondering over the circumstances by which she was surrounded. 'What was that Alice had said, that she so pitied Martin Gurwood? Yes, those were the words, and pity was akin to love.' But the expression on her face when she spoke had, as Pauline had noticed, nothing significant or tell-tale in it. Was there anything in the suspicion concerning Alice and Martin which had once crossed her mind?' She thought not, she hoped not. And yet, what interest had she in that? There was but little chance that this one real passion of her life, her love for this quiet sedate young clergyman, this man so different in manner, thought, and profession from any other she had ever known— there was but little chance that her devotion would be recognised by or even known to him. Well, even in this world justice is sometimes meted out, as Père Gosselin used to tell her—ah, *grand Dieu*, how far away in the mists of ages seem Père Gosselin and the chapel of Notre Dame de la Garde and all the old Marseilles life!—and so she supposes she ought not to expect much happiness, and with a shrug of her shoulders and a wearied sigh, Pauline crept silently to her bed.

*   *   *   *   *

When Mr. Wetter, at the conclusion of his interview with Alice, took his departure from Pollington - terrace, he found himself unexpectedly with some spare time upon his hands. The result of that interview had been so different from what he had anticipated, his preconceived arrangement had been so rudely overthrown, that he was almost unable at first to realise his position, and was in some doubt as to the nature of the next steps it would be best for him to take.

'A most unsatisfactory and ridiculous conclusion,' said he to himself, dropping from the hurried pace at which he had quitted the house into a leisurely amble; 'most unsatisfactory and highly ridiculous, to think that a man of my experience, who has been in the habit of treating matters of this kind for so many years, and with so many different styles of persons, should allow himself to be shut up and put down by that mild-spoken innocent, is beyond all powers of comprehension. I suppose it was because she was innocent that I gave way. I had expected something so completely different, that when it dawned upon me that she was speaking the truth, and that she actually had believed herself to be that old rascal's wife, I was so taken aback, that my usual *savoir-faire* completely deserted me. No doubt about the fact, though I think women's attempts at innocence are generally spoiled by being overdone ; but this seemed in every way to be the genuine article. What a scoundrel must that Calverley have beén! This is just another instance of those men who are so highly respectable, and looked up to as patterns of all the domestic virtues, turning out after death to have been the most consummate hypocrites and shams, and infinitely worse than most of us, who, because we are less circum-spect, have obtained the reputation of being black sheep. I myself never went in for being particularly straitlaced, but certainly I was never guilty of such a cold-blooded piece of villany as that perpetrated by the respectable patriarch of Great Walpole-street.

'What an idiot I was not to have recognised at once that a person of her appearance and manner could not be what she seemed, not to have discovered that she was in a false position, and ignorant herself of what must have been thought about her! Then, of course, I should have approached her in a different manner, made other plans equally easy of execution and far more certain of success. What an idiot I am,' he continued, striking his cane with vehemence against the ground, ' to think about her any more! There are hundreds of women quite as pretty and far more fascinating who would be only too well pleased to receive any attention from me, so why do I worry myself about one who has given me such a decided rebuff. Why? Most likely from the fact that that very rebuff has given piquancy to the adventure, that I am disinclined, because unaccustomed, to sit down under a sense of failure, and because—there!—because she seems to have be-

witched me, and at my time of life, with all
my experience, I am as much in love with
her as if I were a boy suffering under my
first passion.'

With a gesture of contempt for his own
folly Mr. Wetter called a cab, and caused himself to be conveyed to his lodgings in South
Audley-street, whence, at the expiration of a
quarter of an hour, he issued to mount his
horse, which he had ordered to be brought
round to him, and to ride off at a sharp pace.
Whither? With the one idea of Alice domi-
nant in his mind, he thought he would like
to see once more the spot to which his attention had once been attracted; and though
he had not much daylight before him, he
turned his horse's head in the direction of
Hendon.

Daylight was in truth beginning to wane,
and Miss M'Craw, who was true to her old
habits, and kept up as strict a system of es-
pionage upon the family of the American
gentleman, then domiciled in Rose Cottage,
as ever she had upon Alice and John Calver-

ley, was thinking of retiring from her post of observation at the window, when the figures of the horseman and his chestnut thorough-bred, which had formerly been so familiar to her, once more met her view.

Miss M'Craw strained almost out of the window with astonishment. 'What on earth has brought him back after so long an absence?' she said to herself. 'He cannot possibly be going to call upon those horrible American people.'

From her employment of this adjective, it will be gathered that Miss M'Craw did not cherish a particularly friendly feeling towards the new occupants of Rose Cottage. The fact was that her inquisitiveness and propensity to scandal came speedily under the observation of Mr. Hiram B. Crocker, the American gen-tleman in question, who described them under the head of 'general cussedness,' declined the acquaintance of Miss M'Craw, and had huge boardings built up in the corners of his grounds for the purpose of intercepting her virgin gaze.

No, the equestrian was not going to call at Rose Cottage; did not stop at the gate, but

rode slowly on until he reined-in his horse in
the accustomed spot on the brow of the hill,
and raising himself in his stirrups stood for
an instant looking into the garden. He remembered then how he had first seen her
tending her flowers, and looking eagerly out,
evidently awaiting the arrival of some one,
and how in a subsequent ramble he had discovered that some one to be John Calverley of
Great Walpole-street, and all that had happened therefrom.

'How well the cards lay to my hand at
one time,' he said to himself with an impatient
gesture; 'and what a mess I have made of the
game.' And with that he shook his horse's
bridle and cantered away.

When Mr. Wetter reached South Audley-
street, he found his groom standing on the
curbstone, and a gentlemen in the act of
knocking at the door. Alighting, he found
this gentleman, to his great astonishment, to
be Mr. Humphrey Statham; and at sight of
him an uneasy pang shot through Mr. Wetter's
mind. Humphrey Statham was, as he knew,

an intimate friend of Mrs. Claxton's, and his visit there was doubtless on business connected with her. If she had described the scene which had passed between them that morning, that business would doubtless be of a very unpleasant character, and Mr. Wetter was not a brave man physically. He had borne in his time a vast amount of moral obloquy, and borne it well; but he had a horror of anything like physical pain, and Humphrey Statham was a big, strong, and resolute man. No wonder, therefore, that the article which did Mr. Wetter duty for a conscience quailed within him, or that he felt sorely uncomfortable when he recognised the visitor on his doorstep.

But he was the last man to give any early outward sign of such emotion, and it was in sprightly tones and with an air of easy jauntiness that he said,

'My dear Mr. Statham, I congratulate myself immensely on having returned so exactly in the nick of time, if, as I imagine, you were about to do me the honour of paying me a visit.'

'I was coming to call upon you, Mr. Wetter,' said Statham simply.

'Then pray walk in,' said Wetter, opening
the door with his key, and following closely
after him up the stairs. 'Take that chair;
you will find it, I think, a particularly comfortable one; and,' going to an old oak side-
board, 'let me give you an appetiser, a petit
verre of absinthe or vermouth. They are both
here, and either of them is a most delicious
ante-prandial specific.'

'No, thank you,' said Humphrey Statham;
'I will not drink with you.'

Whether intentionally or not, he laid such
stress on the last words that Mr Wetter looked
up at him for an instant with flashing eyes.
But his voice was quite calm when, a minute
after he said, 'I will not attempt to per-
suade you. There is no such mistaken hospi-
tality as that. And now, as a man of your
business habits does not waste his time without a purpose, I will inquire the object of
this visit.'

'It is not one into which business enters,

in the strict sense of the word,' said Statham.

'So much the better,' said Mr. Wetter, with
a gay smile. 'What is not a visit of business
must be a visit of pleasure.'

'I hope you will find it so,' said Statham
grimly. 'Its object, so far as I am concerned,
is very easily stated. You were at Mrs. Claxton's to-day?'

'I was,' said Wetter, putting a bold face
on the matter.

'And when there you thought it expedient
to your purpose, and being expedient for your
purpose, not below your dignity as a man, to
subject your hostess for the time to the gross-
est insult that could be passed upon any one.'

'Sir!' cried Wetter, springing up.

'Be patient, Mr. Wetter, please,' said
Humphrey Statham calmly; 'I have a great
deal more to say. This lady had been made
the victim of a most shameful, most diabolical
fraud—the innocent victim, mind, of a fraud
which robbed her of her good name, and
blasted her position among honest men and

women. She was ignorant as well as innocent, she knew not how basely she had been
deceived; her friends kindly conspired to
hide from her the blackness of her surround-
ings, and to keep her, poor child, in a fool's
paradise of her own. And they succeeded
until you came.'

'I was the serpent, in point of fact, in this
fool's paradise that you speak of.'

'The character fits you to a nicety, Mr.
Wetter, and you kept up the allegory by opening the eyes of the woman and causing her to
know the position she occupied! Which was
a genial, gentlemanly, generous act!'

'Look here,' said Mr. Wetter, 'there is a
certain amount of right in what you say,
though you are sufficiently hard upon me.
But you know all is fair in love.'

'Love!' cried Statham scornfully.

'Well,' said Mr. Wetter, 'it is the most eu-
phonious name for the feeling. All is fair in
love or war, and I give you my word that
when I spoke to Mrs. Claxton, I fully believed
that she knew perfectly well the position she

was occupying, and had accepted it of her
own free will.'

'Do you believe that now?'

'No, I do not. I am a tolerably good
hand at reading character, and there was
something in her look and manner which convinced me that her statement, that she really
believed Calverley to be Claxton, and imagined herself to be his wife, was true.'

'And yet you had the insolence to offer
her—'

'Don't let us use harsh words, please, Mr.
Statham. This is all very fine talking, but
the fact remains the same. This lady was
John Calverley's mistress; nothing can put
that aside or blot that out. What I proposed
to do was, to make her very rich, and happy,
and comfortable. Could a man be found who
would do any more? Is there any one who
would be such a fool as to marry her?'

'Yes,' said Humphrey Statham, rising from
his seat and confronting his companion; 'yes,
Mr. Wetter,' he said, speaking very slowly,
'there is one man whose dearest hope in life

it is to marry Alice Claxton. You are a man of the world, Mr. Wetter, and having said that much, I need add nothing to make you understand that it will be best and safest for you to respect her for the future. I came here this evening to impress this upon you, and having done so, I take my leave. Good-night.'

And as he walked out, he saw by the expression of Mr. Wetter's face that no farther interference on the part of that gentleman was to be looked for.

CHAPTER XI.

THE next morning, at about twelve o'clock, Martin Gurwood arrived in Pollington-terrace, and found Alice alone in the drawing-room.

'I came especially to see you,' he said, after the first greeting, 'and yet I scarcely expected to find you had left your room so early. Yesterday was a day of severe trial to you, dear Mrs. Claxton, but you seem to have gone through it bravely.'

'If I did,' said Alice, with a half-mournful smile, 'I think it must have been owing to my pride. I did not know I possessed any of that quality until there came occasion for its display. But I suffered dreadfully from reaction during the night, and was as low and as hysterical as my worst enemy could wish me.'

'But that feeling has passed away now?'

'O yes; with the morning light came brighter thoughts and better sense; and when your name was announced, I was thinking seasonably enough, as it seemed to me, of the mercy of Providence in giving me such kind friends in the midst of my affliction.'

'I am glad to find you in this frame of mind, dear Mrs. Claxton, as I have come to talk to you on a subject which will require your particular attention.'

His voice faltered as he spoke, and the colour forsook her cheeks as she listened to him.

'My particular attention,' she repeated, with a forced smile. 'It must be something serious, then.'

'It is serious, but not, I hope, distasteful,' said Martin. 'I have been with Mr. Statham this morning. I went to him to give him the opportunity of speaking to me upon a matter which I knew he had most deeply at heart, and which must sooner or later have been broached by him.'

He looked at her keenly, watching the effect of his words. Her face expressed great interest, but no alarm, no regret. He was glad of that, he thought to himself.

'I was with Humphrey for an hour, and when I left him I told him I should come straight to you. Mine is a strange errand, Alice'—it was perhaps the first time he had addressed her by her Christian name, and the word as spoken by him rang musically but mournfully on her ear—'a strange errand for a confirmed old bachelor!'

Alice started at the word.

'Yes,' continued Martin, very pale, but striving hard to smile and to command the inflexions of his voice, ' it is the old story ot people preaching what they never intend to practise. Dear Alice, Humphrey Statham loves you, and I am here to ask you to marry him ?'

Bravely done, Martin, at last! Bravely done, though you were asking for what you knew was equivalent to your death-warrant; bravely spoken, without a break in your voice, though her dear eyes were fixed upon you, and you had taken into yours that little hand which you were urging her to bestow upon another.

Alice was motionless for a moment. Then she drew back, shuddering and crying, 'I cannot, I cannot.'

'Stay, Alice,' said Martin, in his soft soothing tone. 'Humphrey Statham is a great and a good man, and you owe him much. You know that I would not unnecessarily wound your feelings, dear Alice; but I must tell you that when we first discovered who you were, it was entirely owing to Humphrey Statham's chivalry, patience, and good sense that matters were arranged as they were, and that you were up to yesterday kept in ignorance of the fraud which had been practised on you. I, misinformed and bigoted as I was, had intended to take other steps, but I yielded to Humphrey's calm counsel. Ever since that hour he has watched over your best interests with the keenest sympathy. Any comfort you have experienced is due to his fostering care and forethought, and so late as yesterday you yourself heard him plead your cause with eloquence, which was inspired by his affection for you.'

He paused for a moment, and Alice spoke. 'It is not that,' she said; 'it is not that. I know all I owe to Mr. Statham; I have long since acknowledged to myself how kind and good he has been to me. But,' she added, with downcast eyes and flushing cheeks, 'how can I let a man like that take me for his wife? He thinks he loves me now, and doubtless he does. He is not the man to be led away by his feelings, but the love of any man for me would be exposed to a worse trial than that of time or use. Could Mr. Statham bear to know that the world was talking of his wife, to guess what it said? Is not the world filled with persons like Mr. Wetter, and should I not by marrying any honest man expose him to the sneers and gibes of such a crew. I could not do it! I would not do it!'

'There would be no question of that,' said Martin Gurwood. 'Recollect that your story

in its minutest details is known to Mr. Statham, and that he is the last man in the world
likely to act upon impulse, or without a calm
analysis of the motives that prompt him.
There is no one who can testify to this so
strongly as myself, and I can declare to you
solemnly that it was made clear to both of us
long since how blameless you were, and how
grievously you had been sinned against.   Do
not abide by that hastily-spoken decision,
Alice, I beseech you.   Think of what a noble
fellow Humphrey is ; recollect how true and
steadfast and triumphant has been his advo-
cacy of your cause; recollect that he is no
longer young, and that on your reply to the
question I have put to you hangs the hope of
his future life.'

Bravely spoken, Martin!   The work of
expiation progresses nobly now!

Alice was silent for a moment.   Then she
said, 'If I could think this—'

'Think it, believe it, rely on it!   Standing
to you. in the relation which was half self-
assumed, half imposed upon me by the force

of circumstances; loving you, as I do, with a brotherly regard—' (his voice faltered for an instant here; but he quickly regained its command) — 'I could not be blinded in a matter in which your future happiness is involved, even by my affection for Humphrey Statham. Hearing this, you need have no farther fear. See, Alice, I may go back to Humphrey and make him happy, may I not? I may tell him, at least, that there is hope?'

Again a pause. Then the low but clear reply:

'You may.'

'God bless you, dear, for those words!' said Martin, bending down and touching her forehead with his lips. 'They will give new life to the noblest fellow in the world!' Then, as he drew back, he muttered to himself, 'It is all over now.'

'And you,' said Alice, laying her hand gently on his arm, 'you spoke of yourself just now as a confirmed bachelor; but I have had other hopes for you.'

'What do you mean?' he cried.

'Women's eyes are quick in such matters,'
she said. 'Have you been too absorbed to
perceive that there is one by whom your every
movement is watched, your every thought anticipated? one for whose first proofs of kindness to me I was indebted to the interest she
takes in you? one who—'

'I think you must be mistaken, my dear
Alice,' said Martin coldly. 'It has been or-
dained that my life is to be celibate and solitary; and what pleasure I am to have is to
be derived from the contemplation of your
happiness. So be it; I accept my fate. Now
I must hasten back to Humphrey with the
good news.'

He kissed her forehead again, and left the
room. As he passed down the stairs, he saw
through the open door Pauline seated at the
table in the dining-room writing. She looked
up at his approach; and though he had intended going straight out, he could not resist
her implied invitation to speak to her.

'After all, it will be better so,' he said to
himself.

'I thought you would be here this morning, Monsieur Martin,' said Pauline timidly. 'You have seen Alice, and you find her better than we could have hoped for, do you not?'

'Yes,' said Martin, 'I certainly found her better; 'but it was my good fortune to be the bearer of some news to her which I think has left her better still.'

The idea which had haunted her previously—was it true? had he come to make the announcement?

'You the bearer of news?' she asked in tremulous tones.

'Yes,' he replied cheerily; 'good news for Alice, and news in which you, dear Mrs. Durham, will consequently rejoice. There is every reason that you, who have been so faithful to the trust reposed in you, so stanch a friend to us all, should be the first to hear it. Dear Alice is going to be married to Humphrey Statham.'

The tension of suspense had been so great that Pauline had scarcely strength to express her delight.

'Yes,' said Martin, speaking slowly and with emphasis, but purposely averting his eyes from his companion. 'It is a great blessing to me to know that two persons whom I love so dearly will be happy. I daresay it seems strange to other persons, and indeed it does sometimes to myself, to think that I, who am a confirmed bachelor, and who from very early youth determined to lead a single life, can take interest in settling the domestic matters of my friends. But in this instance, at least, I take the greatest interest; and I am sure that you will have the good sense to understand and appreciate my motive.'

'You pay me a great compliment by saying so, Monsieur Martin,' said Pauline in a low constrained voice. Then, after a little pause, she asked, 'Have you five minutes to spare, Monsieur Martin, while I talk to you about myself?'

'Certainly,' said Martin; 'I was on my way to Humphrey with the news.'

'It is good news, and he can wait for it five minutes. If it were bad, it would go to him quickly enough,' said Pauline. 'I will not detain you longer than the time I have mentioned. I told you I wanted to talk to you about myself; and the subject is therefore not one in which I take much pleasure, or, indeed, much interest.'

'You should not speak so bitterly,' said Martin kindly. 'There are two or three of us whose best regard you have won and retain.'

'I did not mean to be bitter, Monsieur Martin,' said Pauline humbly. 'I will put what I have to say in very few words. It will be obvious to you that the time has now arrived when the manner of my life must be again altered. Alice will find, or rather has found, a guardian better able to watch over and protect her; and my part, so far as she is concerned, is played out. You know all my story, Monsieur Martin, and you know human nature sufficiently well to recognise me as a woman of activity, and to be sure that it would be impossible for me to endure the nullity of this English life, in which I have no place; and now that Alice is safe, and going to be happy and respectable for ever, no occupation. I must be kept from thought, too, Monsieur Martin; from thinking of the past—you comprehend that.'

'Not of the immediate past,' he said gently. 'Recollect what use you have been to us: how could we have done without you? It will be pleasant to you to recollect the services you have rendered to this poor girl: how by your aid, at that fearful time of trial in the house at Hendon, we were enabled to overcome the difficulties which arose, and which would have been too much for us, but for your quickness and mother-wit. You will recollect how successfully you have watched over her here, and how her health has suffered but little comparatively from the dreaded shock under your skilful nursing and kind companionship. It will be pleasant to recall all these things, will it not, Pauline?'

'Yes,' said Pauline, pondering; 'but there is another portion of my past upon which I shall not care to dwell. To prevent the thought of that coming over me, and striking sorrow and dismay into my soul, I must give up this dreamy easy-going existence, and take to a life of action. I am not a strong-minded woman, Monsieur Martin; and God knows I do not pretend to have a mission, or any non-sense of that kind. There are not many positions for which I am fitted; some would be beyond my moral, others beyond my physical, strength. But I must have a career of some sort; and away in France there are various means of honest industry for women among my compatriots such as are not to be found here.'

'You intend to leave England, then?' asked Martin.

'Yes,' said Pauline. 'Why should I remain? As I said before, my part here is played out. Do you think it will be long before Alice is married?'

'I cannot say,' said Martin. 'No date has been mentioned; but if I am consulted, I shall advise that the marriage take place as soon as possible. There is no reason for delay; and for my own part, I am anxious to get home again.'

'You will go back to your country parish?' asked Pauline.

'For a time, certainly,' said Martin; 'but my plans are indefinite.'

'On the day of my sister - in - law's marriage, then, when I have placed her in her husband's hands, and thus satisfied myself that she has no farther need of me, I shall bid her adieu, and shall go to France. And I have a request to make to you, Mr. Gurwood, in your position as Mr. Calverley's executor. You are aware that just before I came to reside in his house, I placed in his hands two thousand pounds, which he was good enough to invest for me. I shall now be glad if you will sell those securities, and let me have the money, for which I shall have a use about that time. Will you do so?'

'Certainly I will. But is there no chance of your altering your decision?'

'None. You think it is a right one, do you not?'

'It is a conscientious one, no doubt; but we shall all miss you very deeply.'

Her earnest eyes were fixed upon him as he spoke. His words were fair, as he meant his tone to be hearty and regretful; but he was not clever enough to hide from her his unmistakable pleasure at her decision. She knew that he approved of her departure for Alice's sake, and, bitterest thought of all to her, felt it a relief for his own.

There was an awkward silence for some minutes. To break it, Martin remarked:

'You will be glad to hear that there is no danger of any farther annoyance from Mr. Wetter. It appears that Humphrey saw him yesterday; and after what passed between them, he is perfectly satisfied that Mr. Wetter will not attempt any farther interference.'

'I am pleased to hear it,' said Pauline, 'but not surprised. Henrich Wetter was always a coward; barking loudly when suffered to run at large, but crouching and submissive directly the whip is shaken over him. No, Alice need fear him no more.'

'One word more,' said Martin, rising from his seat; 'one last word, Madame Du Tertre —I shall always think of you by that name, which is very familiar and very pleasant to me—one last word before I take my leave. Can nothing more be done for you to help you in the life which you have chosen?'

Pauline looked at him steadily.

'Nothing,' she replied.

'Recollect that, though I am but a poor country parson, Humphrey Statham is what may be called a rich man; and I am sure I am justified in speaking for him, and saying that any amount of money which you might require would be at your service.'

Pauline shook her head.

'Money in my country, more especially in the southern provinces, where my lot will most probably be cast, goes much farther than it does here; and what I have of my own will enable me not merely to live, but, as I trust, to do a certain amount of good to others. I am very grateful all the same, M. Martin, for your generous offer.'

'My generous offer,' said Martin, 'was simply proposing to acknowledge, in a very slight manner, the existence of a debt due to you by Alice's friends, and which can never be repaid. We will see later on if we cannot induce you to alter your decision.'

'Yes,' said Pauline quietly, 'we will see later on.'

Then Martin Gurwood took his leave of her, and walked back to his hotel. It was nearly over now; he had almost completed his self-appointed task. So well had he performed his mission, that Alice evidently had no idea of the sacrifice he was making in yielding her to his friend, no idea even that he had ever cared for her otherwise than as her guardian. That was proved by the manner in which she had hinted at her hope that he might find solace elsewhere. That was a strange notion too! Could it merely have arisen in Alice's imagination, or was there any real foundation for it? Had he been so absorbed in his infatuation about Alice as to have been blind to all else that was passing round him? He did not know; he could not say. If it was so, he had acted rightly and honestly in the course he had taken with Pauline. His infatuation for Alice! That was all over now: in his intemperate youth he had greatly erred, in his forlorn middle age was he not justly punished?

And while Martin was jostling through the crowd, Pauline sat with her eyes fixed upon the fire, her mind filled with cognate thoughts. To her also the end had come. What had given the relish in her early days had long since grown distasteful to her; and the hope that had proved the light of her later life had, after doubtful flickering, at length been rudely extinguished; and in the hearts both of Martin and Pauline there was the same dismal consciousness that they were justly punished for the misdeeds of their youth, and that their expiation was necessary and just.

Two months after the date of these oc-currences, on a bright and balmy spring morning, at a little City church hiding away somewhere between enormous blocks of warehouses, Humphrey Statham and Alice were married.

Brave to the last, Martin Gurwood performed the service, reading it with a strong manly voice, and imploring the blessing of Heaven on those concerned with unaffected fervour.

When the ceremony was ended, and the bride and bridegroom had departed, Martin joined the one other person who had been present—Pauline.

'Your plans for leaving are matured?' he said.

'So far matured,' she said, with a sad smile, 'that the cab with my luggage is at the end of the street, and that when I leave this, I go on board the steamer.'

'Indeed,' said Martin. 'Then you have taken leave of Alice?'·

'Yes; early this morning.'

'And you have told her of your plans?'

'No, indeed, for they are as yet undecided;

but I have told her that I will write and let her know them.'

'Be sure that you do,' said Martin, 'for we are all of us deeply interested in you. I have brought you,' he added, handing her a packet, 'your own two thousand pounds. With them you will find two thousand pounds more—one thousand from Alice as your sister-in-law, one thousand from Humphrey as your dead husband's old friend. They bade me give you this with their united love, and hoped you would not shrink from accepting it.'

Pauline's voice shook very much as she replied, 'I will accept it certainly; I shall hope to find a good use for it.'

'Of that I have no doubt,' said Martin. They had reached the end of the street by this time, and found the luggage-laden cab in waiting. 'Good-bye, Madame Du Tertre,' said Martin, after he had handed her into the vehicle, 'good-bye, and God bless you.'

'Good-bye, M. Martin,' said Pauline, returning his hand-pressure, and looking for an instant straight into his eyes, 'good-bye.' Then when the cab had driven off, she threw up her hands and crying out passionately, 'Adieu à jamais!' pulled her veil over her face and burst into a flood of tears.

CHAPTER XII.

L'ENVOI.

AWAY in the pleasant village of Twickenham, at the end of a broad lane turning out of the high-road, stands, shut in by heavy iron gates and in the midst of a large and exquisitely-kept garden, a bluff, red-faced, square-built old-fashioned house. From its windows you look across a broad level mead to the shining Thames, winding like a silver thread amongst the rich pasture-grounds, while from the tall elms, planted with forethought more than a century ago to serve as a screen against the north-east wind, comes the cawing of a colony of rooks, who there have established their head-quarters. Over all, house and garden, river and rookery, mead and landscape, there is an air of peace and prosperity, wealth and comfort, calm and repose. Far away on the horizon a lowering gray cloud shows where the great metropolis seethes and smokes ; but so far as freshness and pure air are concerned, you might be in the very heart of the country.

Creeping down the great staircase, and sliding along the broad open balustrade, comes a slim elegant little girl of about eight years old, who slips out through the open dining-room window, and running across the garden to the iron gates, peers long and earnestly down the lane. The little girl is disappointed apparently, for when she turns away, she walks soberly back to the house, and stationing herself at the bottom of the staircase, calls out, 'There is no sign of him yet, papa!'

'Well,' cries a cheery voice from the upper floor, 'there's plenty of time for him to come yet, little Bell! you are such an impatient little woman.' And with these words, Humphrey Statham walks out on to the landing in his dressing-gown, and with a book in his hand.

Three years have passed away since the occurrences narrated in the last chapter. They have left but little mark on our old friend; he is a little more bald, perhaps, and there are, here and there, patches of gray in the roots of his crisp beard, but his eyes are as bright and his manner as cheery as ever.

'You are such an impatient little woman,' he repeated, pulling the child towards him and kissing her forehead.

'No, I am not,' said Bell; 'not impatient generally, pappy, only I want to see the gentleman, and you never will talk to me when you've got a book in your hand.'

'Between you and your mamma, what is one to do?' said Humphrey Statham, laughing. 'Mamma wants me to read to her, you want me to play with you, and it is impossible to please both at the same time.'

'We both want you, because we're both so fond of you, pappy darling,' said Bell, putting up her face again to be kissed, 'and you ought to be pleased at that. There, I declare then I did hear wheels.' And the child breaks away from Humphrey's grasp, and again rushes to the gate.

She is right this time. A fly is driving away, and the gentleman who has alighted from it stands waiting for admittance. A man with a thin face, clean-cut features, and light hair, dressed entirely in black and with a deep mourning band round his hat. He started violently at the sight of the child, but recovered himself with an effort.

'You are little Bell?' he said, putting out his hand.

'Yes,' she replied, sliding her little fingers into his, and looking up fearlessly into his face. 'I am little Bell, and you are Mr. Gurwood. I know you! Papa and mamma have been expecting you, O, ever so long.'

The child pulled him gently towards the house, and he had scarcely crossed the threshold when he was seized in Humphrey Statham's hearty grasp.

'Martin, my dear old friend—at last. We thought you would never come, we have waited for you so long.'

'So Bell tells me,' said Martin, returning his friend's pressure; 'but you see here I am. You're not looking a bit changed, Humphrey! And your wife?'

'Alice! Here she is to answer for herself.'

Yes, she was there, more lovely than ever, Martin thought, in the mellowed rounded beauty of her form, and with the innocent trusting expression in her eyes still unchanged.

Let us, unseen by them, stand by the two old friends as they sit that evening over their wine, in the broad bay-window looking towards the sunset, and from their conversation glean our final records.

'And you are very happy, Humphrey?' asked Martin.

'Happy!' cried Humphrey Statham; 'my dear Martin, I never knew what happiness was before. I rather think,' he continued, with a smile, 'that laziness may have something to do with it. You see, Alice doesn't care much about my being absent for the whole of the day, as I should necessarily be if I attended

strictly to business; and as, living as we do, I
do not spend anything like my income, I
have knocked off City work to a certain extent, and leave the business in Mr. Collins's
charge. He sees how matters are tending,
and has made overtures to buy it, and shortly
I shall let him have it to himself, I suppose.
Not that my life is wholly objectless; there's
the garden to look after, and Bell's education
to superintend, and Alice to be read to; and
then at night I potter away at a book on Maritime Law, which I am compiling, so that I
find the twenty-four hours almost too short
for what I have to do.'

'And Alice?'

'I think that I may say she is perfectly
happy. I have not a thought which she
does not share, not a wish which is not inspired by her.'

'And little Bell? What a charming child
she has grown to be! To go back, Humphrey,
for the first and only time to that conversation which we had in your chambers, I may
say that circumstanced as I am in regard to

that child, I was delighted to notice the fancy she seemed to take to me to-day.'

'Curiously enough she has had from the first mention of your name an odd interest about you, and has frequently asked when you were coming to see us.'

'Does—does Alice know anything about that story?'

'Only so far as I am concerned. I told her of my early attachment to Emily Mitchell, and the story of how I lost her; but she has not the least idea of Emily's farther career beyond the fact that Bell is Emily's child.'

'True to the last, true as steel!' said Martin Gurwood, grasping his friend's hand.

'And now tell me of yourself, Martin,' said Humphrey Statham; 'what you are doing, what are your plans?'

'It is soon told,' said Martin Gurwood. 'I wrote you of my poor mother's death, and told you that she died without making any will. I am consequently her sole heir, and am a very rich man. The money is no good to me, Humphrey, but it will be a fine portion for little Bell, whom I have made my heiress under your guardianship.'

'Time enough to think of that, Martin. What do you intend to do now?'

'To work, old friend, according to my lights, in striving to better the condition of my fellow men. Yesterday I resigned the Vicarage of Lullington, and—'

'You don't mean to say you are going to become a missionary?'

'Not as you seem to suspect,' said Martin, with a smile, 'among savages and cannibals, but among those who perhaps need it not less, the lower classes of London. In striving to do them good, I purpose to spend my life and my income, and it will need but a very moderate amount of success to convince me that I have done rightly.'

'It is not for me to quarrel with the decision, Martin,' said Humphrey Statham; 'it is boldly conceived, and I know will be thoroughly carried out. And it will be moreover a satisfaction to me and to Alice to know that the scene of your labours is so close to us.

When you want temporary rest and change, you will find your home here. You know that there is no one in the wide world whom it would give my wife and myself so much pleasure to welcome.'

'I know it,' said Martin, 'and have my greatest pleasure in knowing it. Now tell me, Humphrey, has anything ever been heard of Madame Du Tertre, of Pauline?'

'Nothing,' replied Humphrey Statham, shaking his head; 'as you know, she promised to write to us to tell us of her plans, but she has never done so, and that, I think, is the one grief of Alice's life. Pauline was so true a friend to my wife at a time when she most needed such a friend, that she was most desirous to hear of her again. But it seems as though that were not to be; her name is one of those which are "writ in water."'

One more look around ere the curtain falls. See Alice adored by her husband, happy and contented with all the troubles of the past obliterated. See Humphrey Statham devoted to his wife, and finding in her love a recompense for the havoc and the tempest which destroyed his early hope. See Martin Gurwood labouring manfully, steadfastly, among the London poor, inculcating both by precept and example the doctrine to the setting forth of which he has devoted his life. See him making occasional holiday with his old friends, and watching over the growth and education of little Bell; thinking of the providence which has endowed this girl so nobly by the hands of the two men who made the story of her mother's life; how sheltered she is, how safe from the terrible temptations which come to women with poverty and friendlessness; how the Yellow Flag will never flaunt over her beautiful head, a taunt and a warning.

THE END.

LONDON:
ROBSON AND SONS, PRINTERS, PANCRAS ROAD, N.W.